Fern Valley Ventures

By

Elizabeth Dooley

Dedication

To David, Sara, and Saffy.

Acknowledgments

'Thank you to Peter, Stephen and Gilly for your kind support and encouragement'.

TABLE OF CONTENTS

About The Author

As a child growing up in the suburbs of Manchester, England, there was nothing more Elizabeth liked to do than curl up with an exciting adventure story. Freedom to roam and play in the fields and woods near her home fuelled her adventurous spirit. Reading continued to feature large as she studied English at Leicester University and then went on to teach in Primary schools. Having married, and with three small children, her taste for adventure was satisfied by living for ten years in Chile, South America, where she wrote a book about the British pioneers of sheep farming in the wilds of Patagonia. Back where she grew up, and now with three grandchildren, she continues to love stories, including those found in the Bible. In writing Fern Valley Ventures she has fulfilled her desire to write wholesome modern adventure stories for children.

The Vanishing

Chapter One: Freedom!

The summer holidays were here at last and the children of Fern Valley Primary couldn't wait to get home.

"At last!" thought Tom. "Now I can really get on with building my tree house with Ali. School takes up so much time, but now we're free. Hurray!"

Tom raced across the playground to his Mum and little sister Pip, looking round impatiently for his best friend Ali. Just then he rushed up, his jolly face beaming with pleasure.

"Come on," he said, "let's get home; it's the holidays."

The two boys retrieved their scooters from the scooter park and sped off along the pavement, skilfully avoiding everything and everyone in their path. So began the long hot summer of freedom - and adventures Tom never could have imagined.

Tom and Ali lived on the same street, just three houses apart. It was a quiet, leafy road with not much traffic. Although their front gardens were small, their back gardens were large and long and best of all ran down to a little hedge of bushes and small trees. On the other side of the hedge was Fern Valley itself. It was a glorious place of untidy patches of grass, ferns, weeds and wild flowers. There were trees and bushes, hollows and hummocks. It had once been the site of an old paper mill which had fallen into disrepair and all that was left were the overgrown remains of broken down walls. The whole place was a fantastic area to play in. It was safe and enclosed but was ideal for hiding, climbing and making dens.

This summer was the first time Tom's and Ali's parents were letting them play there by themselves, without adults and older brothers and sisters to keep an eye on them. Tom and Ali could hardly wait to take off their uniforms and get into their scruffiest clothes because they had big plans. They planned to build a tree house in Fern Valley and couldn't wait to get started.

The boys had been making plans for months. They had already chosen the tree. It was in the far corner of Fern Valley, as far away from their houses as possible. It was quite tall, and the lowest branches were well out of reach of even the tallest person. The trunk branched out into four strong, sturdy branches, ideal for laying the floor of the house. All through winter and spring they had been secretly gathering materials. In his shed Tom had found a large ball of string, some long nails and a hammer which he had hidden behind a roll of old carpet in the garage. Best of all, Ali had found and hidden two large sheets of plywood which were left over from their new kitchen. They would be ideal for the floor of the tree house and one evening, when everyone was watching the telly, he and Tom had dragged them down to the bottom of the garden and hidden them under the hedge. A few weeks ago Tom's parents had re-decorated the lounge and put up new curtains and laid a new carpet. Of course, on the lookout for his tree house, Tom had managed to get some of the old carpet and one of the curtains and hide them at the back of his bedroom cupboard. No one seemed to notice that only one curtain and not much carpet went to the tip.

And now it was the holidays and they could put their plans into operation. But there was one main difficulty. How were they going to keep their tree house a secret? Tom's brother Paul was the main problem. He would see Tom and Ali going into Fern Valley every day and wonder what they were doing. What if he followed them to find out their secret? He would do it just to be annoying, not because he wanted to join in. Paul had played in Fern Valley when he was younger and now thought it was babyish. He would rather play football with his friends in the park, or go skate-boarding or bike-riding, but he could easily poke his nose in and snoop around, just to be awkward. He would make fun of their plans and tell his friends and they would come and laugh and spoil it all.

"What shall we do about Paul?" asked Tom. "He could ruin everything. He could tell Mum and Dad that we've taken things to build our house. He could really get us into trouble."

"I know, said Ali. "We could tell him we're making a garden; you know, getting rid of weeds and planting flowers. He'll think that's so boring and babyish he won't even bother coming to look."

"That's a great idea," replied Tom. "We could even take a spade and fork and start making a garden near the hedge, so if he comes to look he'll see it and go away laughing."

"Yes," said Ali, and if my little sister peers over the hedge that's what she'll see too." Aisha was only six and wasn't allowed in Fern

Valley but she was very nosy and always wanted to know what her big brother was doing.

"Ok," said Tom, "we'll start tomorrow."

Chapter Two: Into Action

The next day after breakfast the two boys told their Mums they were going to play in Fern Valley. Surprisingly Paul showed no interest and went off to play football with his friends, Aisha had a friend round to play and Pip was too small to go anywhere. The coast was clear! Tom got the carpet pieces and curtains out of the cupboard and when his mother was hoovering, smuggled them out of the house and down to the bottom of the garden. He got the hammer, nails and string from the garage and took them to the hedge where they had hidden the plywood. Ali borrowed some gardening tools from his shed so they could start on their pretend garden.

It was all jolly hard work and they hadn't even started building! As they sat at the bottom of the garden having a drink and a rest before the building began, Aisha and her friend appeared.

"What are you doing, Ali? Can we help?" they asked.

"No, go away," Ali and Tom both shouted at the same time. "You know you're not allowed in Fern Valley, you're too little. Go and play somewhere else," added Ali.

The little girls were startled and tears filled their eyes. Aisha wasn't used to being yelled at by her brother, he was usually really nice to her. She wondered what the boys were up to.

"We're going to make a garden in the valley," said Tom. "Look, here are the spade and fork, now go away." Disappointed the girls went back up the garden towards the house and the boys leapt up.

"Phew, that was close," said Ali. "We really will have to start the garden, just to keep the girls away, as well as Paul. This is going to be hard work."

"Yes," said Tom. "But let's get all the stuff over to the tree and start building now. The girls won't be back for a while and we can make a start on the garden later."

They hauled the plywood, carpet, curtain and tools over the rough grass, up and down the hills to the far corner of the valley. Tom was stung on the arm when he brushed past a huge clump of nettles and Ali's foot got stuck in a rabbit hole and he twisted his ankle quite badly. This wasn't turning out to be much fun. Then they realised that there was no way they could get the plywood up to the branches where they would lay it flat for the floor of their house – it was far too high up.

"We'll have to get some step ladders," gasped Tom.

"There are some in my garage," replied Ali, wincing with pain – his ankle really did hurt. "But how are we going to get them here without anyone noticing?"

"I think," replied Tom, "that we're going to have to wait until later, say after tea tonight when they'll all be watching the telly and won't notice."

"I suppose so, but it's really annoying. I wanted to get the house built today," moaned Ali.

"I know, but we'll just have to be patient. Let's start on our pretend garden so Aisha and Paul will see it when they peer over the hedge to have a nosy," suggested Tom.

"Ok, but I hate gardening," sighed Ali.

"Me too," said Tom, "but it's got to be done; come on, let's get going."

So they left everything at the foot of the tree, hidden behind the trunk and went back to the hedge. Ali was hobbling and Tom's arm was burning; this was going to be harder than they had first thought, but they were determined to carry on. And so it was that when Aisha appeared to tell them it was time for lunch, she found them red faced, sweating and dirty, digging and pulling up weeds, clearing the ground for their pretend garden.

At lunch Tom sat down feeling frustrated and dejected.

"How's the garden going?" Paul asked with a laugh.

"Oh, you're making a garden? How lovely!" said Mum. "I didn't know you were interested in gardening. I've got some little plants you can put in. They're all sorts of bright colours and will look lovely!"

"Thank you," mumbled Tom. "Bother," he thought, "we're going to be spending so much time on this jolly garden, we'll never get the tree house built."

The afternoon was spent with more digging and weeding until they thought they had done enough to show anyone peering over the hedge that they really were creating a beautiful garden.

Chapter Three: A Little Lie

They finished work early and planned to meet at Ali's shed at seven o'clock, to take the step ladders when everyone would be watching the television. Tom wondered how he was going to explain where he was going at that time. His Dad would be home from work by then and what was Tom going to say to him? He loved his Dad and he didn't want to tell him even a little lie. So what excuse was he going to make for going to Ali's? He decided to almost tell the truth.

So after dinner he said, "Dad, Ali asked if I could go round to his house to help him with something. Is that alright?"

"What at this time?" replied Dad, "Can't it wait till the morning?"

"Well not really, Ali wants help with it now and it might be too late tomorrow."

"Whatever is he doing that is so urgent and needs your help?" asked Dad.

"Oh just something I'm helping him to make," Tom replied vaguely. "I'll be really quick. Oh please can I go?"

"Ok, but I want you back by 7.30."

"Thanks, Dad, I won't be long." And with that he slipped out of the house. As he jogged over to Ali's, Tom had the strangest feeling that his Dad knew that he hadn't been quite telling the truth but had let him go anyway. But he soon shrugged off the feeling; they had work to do. Ali was already by the shed, trying to unlock the padlock on the door. He was nervous and in a hurry and he kept dropping the key.

"We've got to hurry," he muttered, "Mum will be out to get the washing in soon and she'll see us."

Tom looked down the garden to the house and saw Ali's Mum lit up by the kitchen light, walking backwards and forwards.

"Quick, give me the key," he said.

He was surprised how quickly he managed to undo the lock and open the shed door. It was nearly dark but in the gloom of the shed they could see the step ladders propped up against the wall. Ali dived into the shed and grabbed the step ladders, but at the same time knocked over a pile of paint tins. There was a fearful clatter and they saw Ali's Mum stop and peer out through the window towards them. They managed to get the ladders out and the lock fastened just before Ali's Mum came out into the garden with a laundry basket. The two boys froze in horror; she was going to see them and catch them red-handed. But she was too busy taking the washing off the line, folding it and putting it in the basket. Very slowly and carefully they carried the ladders past the shed and hid them behind the hedge in the long grass. No one would see them before they got them in the morning. Tom realised he was sweating and his heart was racing. He looked at his watch, it was already 7.25!

"I must go now or my Dad will be out looking for me; see you in the morning," he whispered. He raced back to his house and in through the back door. Somehow he didn't want to meet his Dad face-to-face just then.

"I'm back," he called and crept upstairs to his room. Half an hour later when his Dad came up he was surprised to find Tom already showered, in his pyjamas and in bed reading.

"Well, you're in bed early," he laughed. "Did you help Ali?"

"Er yes," said Tom and then quickly changed the subject. "Can we carry on reading my library book please, Dad?"

Twenty minutes later, as he lay drifting off to sleep, Tom thought of all the exciting days which lay ahead him of him and Ali in Fern Valley.

Chapter Four: The Tree House is built

The next morning the boys were out early and soon had the step ladders up against the tree. Ali climbed to the top and Tom managed to pass the first of the plywood boards up to him. Then holding the board, Ali climbed up to where the four branches spread out. Dragging the wood up behind him he laid it flat on the branches and found it was a perfect fit. They did the same with the second board and then Tom climbed up the ladder with the nails and hammer in his pockets. Ali was already standing on the boards and they made a perfect floor for their tree house. Although it wasn't wobbly they decided to hammer a few nails through the boards into the branches, just to fix the floor firmly.

It was harder than they thought and it took a lot of hammering. Once Ali dropped the hammer and Tom had to climb down and get it from the long grass and of course one of them was going to hit his thumb with the hammer – it was Tom. It hurt so much and even though he tried to be brave, a few tears trickled down his face. But it was all worth it. The floor was firm and strong and gave them a lot of space. All they had to do now was lay the carpet and hang the curtain up to make the walls. But just as Tom was climbing down to get the carpet he heard his mother calling.

"Tom, I've brought the plants for your garden. Where are you?"

"Quick," hissed Tom, "if we're not careful she'll come looking for us and see the tree house." They scrambled down the ladder so quickly that they both scraped their hands and bumped their knees – more injuries to add to their collection.

"Hurry, take the ladder down and throw it in the bushes," whispered Ali. They had only just hidden the ladder and started walking away from the tree when they saw Tom's Mum coming towards them.

"Oh there you are! What are you doing here?" she asked. "I thought you were doing your garden."

"Oh, we were just having a rest and wandering round a bit," said Tom vaguely, hoping she couldn't see the tree with the floor nailed to its branches just behind them.

"Well you're certainly looking dirty," she remarked, looking at their hot, sweaty faces and scruffy jeans. "You must have been working hard in your garden. I've left you the little plants over here." She turned back towards the hedge and much relieved, the boys followed her away from the tree house.

"Thanks Mum," said Tom, trying to sound enthusiastic, "we can put them in now." Picking up their trowels they began digging holes for the pansies, begonias and yellow daisies. Tom's Mum returned to the garden calling over her shoulder, "Lunch will be in about an hour, don't be late."

"Phew, "gasped Ali, "that was close. I thought she was getting suspicious and was going to ask questions."

"Yes, we'd better plant all these now or she really will wonder what we are up to," sighed Tom. They worked quickly, digging small holes and stuffing the plants in.

"We'll have to get some water for them," said Ali.

"Yes," said Tom, "after lunch we can bring down a watering can for the plants and then we can finish off the house."

After lunch they stumbled back to Fern Valley with a very full watering can. They had to take turns carrying it and water slopped over their jeans and trainers making them feel damp and uncomfortable. But that was soon forgotten as they watered in the new plants and then hurried on to finish the tree house. Soon the carpet was laid on the wooden boards, string was tied from branch to branch and the old curtain was hung over to make walls like a tent. They hammered the curtain to the edges of the floor leaving only one flap open at the front to use as the door. Once they had finished they sat snugly in their new den and admired their handiwork.

"This is fantastic," said Tom. "We can come here all summer. Let's bring some food and drink and things to play with."

"Yes, and what about some cushions and blankets? We can make it so cosy up here," suggested Ali, and Tom agreed.

Chapter Five: Home from Home

The next day they made many secret trips from home to the tree house, each time smuggling something new to make their house a home. Ali managed to get two cushions and an old picnic blanket which he found in the cupboard under the stairs. Tom found two old, chipped cups and plates at the back of a kitchen cupboard. They both brought books, toys and games from their bedrooms and biscuits and juice from their kitchens. No one seemed to notice their frequent comings and goings and if they did, they made no comment. The boys were relieved to find that everyone seemed to have lost interest in their activities in Fern Valley. Their brother and sisters were all interested in their own friends and their mothers seemed rushed off their feet doing the things mothers do. Their tree house was a club house, or a helicopter, or a police car, or a space ship. There seemed to be no end to the games they could play there; but best of all was when it was just their den and they could hide away in secret.

But after a few days Tom began to wish there were more children to play with. Only two people in a club seemed small and how could you have The Fern Valley Gang of only two? One afternoon as they were up in the house nibbling biscuits, he suggested to Ali that they let a few more children into their secret and invite them into the gang.

"What about the twins," he suggested, "or Jim? And Laura and Amelia are quite good fun."

But Ali did not agree.

"They might take over our den and spoil our games. What if they boss us about? It won't be just ours anymore," he protested.

Tom was prepared to risk that. "But it'll be more interesting and exciting with more of us; it won't get boring."

"Boring?" cried Ali jumping up. "You mean you're bored with me? Well if you feel like that I'm going home and you can invite all your stupid friends. I thought you were my friend. I thought we were having fun together." Tears of anger streamed down his red cheeks as he grabbed some of his things and started down the ladder.

"No, don't go, of course I'm your friend, you're my best friend. We won't invite anyone else if you don't want," Tom pleaded.

But it was too late. Ali stormed across the valley, heading for home. As he got to the little garden he kicked some of the plants and sent their petals flying everywhere.

"Come back," called Tom, but Ali had disappeared through the hedge. Tom felt so miserable; he hadn't meant to hurt Ali, but he really did think that a few more friends would liven things up. He decided he didn't like secrets; surely it was best to share good things with your friends? He especially wanted to show the tree house to his Dad. He would think it was great and would probably think of a few improvements they could make. They really needed help making steps up to the house – perhaps a rope ladder they could pull up once they were inside so no one could get in when they were there. As it was, they had to leave the step ladder against the tree trunk and anyone could climb up it and into the house.

Suddenly the tree house didn't seem fun anymore. Tom climbed down the ladder and threw it behind the tree. What was he going to do now? Ignore Ali and tell their friends about their den, but then Ali might never be his friend again? Or apologise to him and promise to keep the secret to themselves? Everything had gone wrong.

Tom picked up a big stick and started to slash angrily at the brambles, weeds and nettles around him. There was a particularly big clump of brambles and Tom started to attack it, hacking away at the prickly stems and leaves. As he did so he noticed that they were covering up a hole in the ground. Around the hole, bricks were scattered about and Tom realised that this must be the remains of the old mill buildings, fallen down and overgrown. He peered more closely and saw that through the hole were some steps leading down.

Very cautiously, taking care not to get scratched by the brambles, Tom stepped towards the hole. He used his stick to hold back the prickly branches but even so could feel his jeans getting caught and then there was a tearing sound and he saw a big rip in his jeans. He thought what a good job that they were an old pair. He wasn't worried about tears and scratches, he was too excited. He had found something that had been hidden for ages which no one knew about. This was even better than the tree house. He reached the hole and saw the steps leading down into the darkness. Very slowly and carefully, he put his foot on the first step, and as it seemed safe he carried on down. The further down he got, the darker it became until he was in the pitch black. He looked back and saw a circle of light shining above him. It was about ten steps until he reached the bottom and under his feet he could feel the hard floor. It smelled dusty and musty but seemed clean and dry. Tom realised that he had found a fantastic hiding place that no one knew about; not even Ali. He decided he would come back the next day with a torch and explore properly. Climbing back up the steps, he pushed through the brambles – oops another tear in his jeans and ouch, more scratches on his hands and arms. Using the stick, he carefully pushed everything back over the hole and checked that no one could see it. By the time he got back to the hedge, not only were his jeans torn, but he realised his hands and arms were covered in itchy scratches.

"Long sleeves, gloves and a torch are what I'll need tomorrow," he thought. He decided to get some of the more important things from the tree house in case it rained or someone came snooping around. Then he quickly put the plants that Ali had kicked away back into the soil. He slipped back into the house, changed his jeans and put on a long sleeved top to cover his scratched arms.

"I'll go round to Ali's tomorrow and say I'm sorry," he thought, "but I'm not going to tell him about the hole in the ground, not yet."

Chapter Six: A Surprise and a Day Out

When he got to Ali's house the next morning he found the family packing the car with cases and bags. He was so surprised that he forgot the argument from the day before.

"What's happening?" he asked Ali who was just coming out of the house looking clean and tidy and with his back pack on his back.

He looked a bit flustered, "Oh!" he said. "My Mum just got a last minute deal on a holiday so we're going to Spain for two weeks!"

Tom was stunned, "What am I going to do without you for two weeks? What about our tree house?"

"I know," said Ali, "and I'm sorry about yesterday. I'm sorry for being so silly; of course you can invite other people to the den, especially as I'll be away for so long."

"Well, I don't know now," said Tom. "I was coming round to say that you were right – it should just be our secret."

"Time to go now," called Ali's Mum. "Hop into the car, Ali."

Climbing into the back seat Ali whispered, "Its ok, just invite one or two of our friends to keep you company. What about the twins Jackie and Jill? They'd be good fun and they can keep a secret."

Tom hardly had time to agree and wish Ali a good time before his Dad had switched on the engine and the car sped off up the road. Tom stood waving, then walked slowly back home deep in thought. How quickly things changed. One minute he and Ali had a fantastic secret tree house together, the next they had argued about it and now Ali wasn't even going to be there for ages. At least they were friends again and Tom wondered once more about his idea of inviting Jackie and Jill and some others to the house. The twins were the same age as them and lived on the same road but they were a bit bossy and always wanted to play games their way. Perhaps Ali was right and they would end up feeling like guests in their own home. He decided he would have to give it some more thought.

When he got home he was surprised to find that his Dad hadn't gone to work. He was smiling and ruffled Tom's hair, "Good news," he said. "I've taken a couple of days off work and today we've decided to have a family day out. We thought about going to Timmin's Farm and Park; Mum's making the picnic now."

Tom was thrilled, "Can we take the cricket set and the Frisbee and the kite and…...."

"Slow down," laughed Dad, "Go and get what you want and we'll see if we can fit it in. We've got to take Pip's push chair and Paul wants to take the fishing tackle and of course there's the picnic basket and blankets."

Within half an hour the car was loaded up and they were ready for off. Everyone was in a good mood, the sun was shining and Tom forgot all about Ali and the tree house; this was going to be a great day out.

They hadn't gone far when Dad said, "I'm a bit short of cash. We'd better stop and get some from the hole in the wall outside the bank. Who wants to come with me?"

"Me please," said Tom. He loved watching money appear as if by magic from the ATM when Dad just pressed a few buttons. This time he watched carefully as Dad put his purple bank card in a slot which gobbled it up and then pressed four numbers, 0412.

"Gosh," thought Tom, "that's my birthday, the 4th of December. Dad must use my birthday to work the machine."

As the ten brown notes slipped out of another slot and his Dad put them in his wallet with his card, Tom noticed something amazing. On the machine above his head was a sign which read

"FREE CASH WITHDRAWALS"

He hadn't realised you could get free money from these machines; what a great idea! He was just about to say something to his Dad when they heard the car horn and saw his Mum waving frantically. Tom realised they had parked at a bus stop and a bus was coming. They raced back to the car and sped off just before the bus drew up.

They had such a great day out. There were no arguments, the picnic was delicious and there had been lots of things to see at the farm; but most of all Tom enjoyed the time spent playing with his Dad. He was always so much fun to be with and you could have a real laugh with him.

On the way home Tom wondered if he would invite Jackie and Jill into the tree house. He decided that he might, but first of all he was going to explore his even greater secret: the underground room hidden by brambles from everyone's sight but his own.

Chapter Seven: Into the Dark

The next day his Dad was still at home and the morning was spent helping him in the garden. Tom had almost given up on getting into Fern Valley at all that day when he heard his parents planning to visit the big out-of-town furniture store to look at a dining room table and chairs.

"Gran will come and look after you and Pip," said Mum, "and Paul is going with his friend Pete and his parents to a basketball game."

Normally Tom would have felt annoyed at being left at home with his little sister, even though it was Gran who was looking after them – she was usually good fun. But today he knew it would give him the chance to slip out for a bit to explore the underground room. He was pleased to see Gran when she arrived and enjoyed chatting and playing together. He was getting pretty good at Scrabble and won the game but was annoyed with Pip when she won a game of Snakes and Ladders. She couldn't even count and move her counter along properly but every time she threw the dice she landed at the foot of a ladder and shot up it, whereas whenever it was his turn he landed on a snake's head and was soon back to square one. So annoying! Gran reminded him it was just a game of luck with no skill involved and that he had used his brains to win at Scrabble. Usually he enjoyed playing these old-fashioned games with Gran but today he felt impatient to be outside. Gran said it was fine for him to go into the garden for a bit but did look a bit surprised when she saw he had taken off his shorts and T-shirt and put on thick jeans and a long-sleeved jumper.

"Won't you be too hot, Tom?" she asked. "It's a very warm afternoon." He pretended not to hear her and just smiled and waved as he went out of the back door.

"She'd be even more surprised if she knew I had a pair of woolly gloves stuffed in my pockets," he thought.

When he was sure Gran was back in the sitting room watching the telly with Pip, Tom hurried down the garden, through the hedge and into Fern Valley. He poured some more water on the little plants as he passed and then hurried over to the tree house where he remembered he had left the torch. It took him no time at all to climb the ladder and retrieve it from the little pile of belongings that were still there. Pulling on his gloves and finding a long strong stick, he pushed back the brambles and could soon see the hole and the steps leading down into darkness. It was so much better with long sleeves and gloves and soon he was through the brambles without one scratch. Switching on the torch, he shone it onto the ten steps and was soon down them and into the room. He shone the torch around, up and down, round and round and gasped. The room was even better than he had hoped. It was about the size of his bedroom, with a low ceiling and a wide wooden bench running along one of the walls. Everything was dusty but it was dry and cosy.

"I could even live here," he thought, and there and then he decided to make it his home. He would leave the tree house as it was and invite his friends to play with him there, but absolutely no one would know about the secret times he would spend here alone.

Hurrying back up the steps, carefully replacing the brambles, his head was spinning with plans. He would need his sleeping bag, bottles of water, food, batteries for the torch, perhaps the big camping lamp if he could find it and warm clothes in case it got cold.

He slipped back into the house and up the stairs, listening out for Gran and Pip who were laughing at one of Pip's favourite cartoons. Wasting no time he got his sleeping bag from the cupboard and stuffed as many clothes as he could into his back pack. Into a couple of plastic bags he put a pillow, a few books and some paper and a pen. Hiding them in the bottom of his cupboard, he decided he would take them to his new hide-out tomorrow, together with some food and drink.

It was hard to hide his excitement, but by the time his parents were back and Gran had gone home, he had changed his clothes and was ready to sit down and eat with the family. They had got take away pizza and chips and it should have been a really enjoyable treat, but something was wrong. His parents looked unhappy and kept on snapping at each other, even though they kept smiling at the children and pretending to be cheerful. Even when Dad read Tom a chapter of his book and tucked him up in bed and told him a new 'Knock knock' joke, Tom thought he looked a bit sad.

"Night Dad, love you," he said as he snuggled under the duvet.

"Love you too," said Dad, "always will."

Instead of falling asleep, Tom lay awake; his head whirling with plans for his new hide out. But as he lay there he heard raised voices from down stairs; first his Mum and then his Dad and each time their voices got louder and angrier. Tom opened his bedroom door and crept onto the landing. He could hear quite clearly now.

"You know we can't afford that furniture," said Dad, "it's just too extravagant."

"But it's solid oak, it will last us forever and it's so beautiful," Mum said.

"I don't care if it's made out of solid gold, "Dad shouted. "We haven't got enough money and that's that."

Tom shut his bedroom door and crept miserably back to bed. He couldn't stand his parents arguing and he buried his head under the duvet. The argument went on for ages but eventually doors banged, lights went out and his parents stomped off to bed. As he lay there in the dark it was then he had his brilliant idea. Why were they worrying about money when they could go to the cash machine and get free cash? It was easy. He would take Dad's card out of his wallet, go into town to the cash machine, get some of the free money and give it to his Mum so she could have the furniture she wanted. He just didn't know why Dad hadn't thought of it already! With that in mind he was soon fast asleep.

Chapter Eight: Free Money

Despite his late night Tom was up early to put his plan into action. And it was all so easy. His Dad was going back to work today and Tom knew he always left his wallet with the card in at home in his bedside table drawer. So far, so good. After breakfast Mum said they would have to go to the supermarket to do the weekly shop and Tom knew there was one of those free cash machines just outside the shop. Slipping up to his parents' room he found his Dad's wallet and the purple card in it. He got it out and putting the card in his pocket, he returned the wallet to the drawer.

Everything went smoothly. The supermarket was huge and it was easy for him to wander off from Mum who was pushing Pip in the trolley and race outside to the machine. Remembering what his father had done, he put in the card, punched in 0412 and then panicked. How much money should he get? Someone was coming up behind him so he hurriedly pressed some numbers. Piles of purple notes came flooding out of the slot and the card shot out of the other hole. Quickly he stuffed all the money into both pockets of his jeans; there did seem to be a lot of it. Racing back into the shop he found his Mum searching in the freezer cabinet for Pip's favourite fish fingers.

"Where did you get to?" his mother said vaguely, "I thought you'd got lost." She didn't seem to expect an answer and soon Tom was helping her pack the shopping into bags and load it into the car.

Back at home he helped her unload the bags and then went upstairs. First he returned the card to his Dad's wallet and then went into his bedroom, shutting the door firmly and then leaning against it.

He certainly didn't want Pip or his Mum barging in. Carefully he pulled all the notes out of his pockets and laid them flat on the floor in a pile. He saw they were all £20 notes. Slowly he started to count them. It was only when he had counted out fifty notes and then counted them again to make sure he was right, that he realised he had £1,000 in his bedroom! He began to panic; he really hadn't meant to take so much. In his hurry he must have pressed the wrong numbers. Were you really allowed to take so much free money? He began to doubt whether it really was free after all. He put all the money between the pages of the biggest book he had, a large children's encyclopaedia, and hid it in a drawer under his winter jumpers. He wasn't sure what to do with it now. Perhaps his Mum wouldn't be as pleased as he had thought she would be. She was calling him down for lunch and he went downstairs trying not to look guilty and afraid.

After lunch Pip was having a friend round to play whose mother was coming too. All four of them would be busy chatting and playing. Tom told his Mum he would be fine by himself. As soon as the visitors had arrived he changed into his long sleeved top and old jeans.

It took him three trips to carry all the bags from his room into Fern Valley. It was lucky they had just been to the supermarket as there was plenty of food and drink to help himself to from the kitchen. He packed four plastic bags with biscuits, crackers, bread rolls, a jar of jam, a cake and two big bottles of lemonade. He remembered to take a knife, fork, cup and plate too. It took several trips to carry the bags over the hedge and one time Pip and her friend came out into the garden and watched him struggling with one of the bags. He told them fiercely to go away and, rather startled, they went back into the house.

Once he had got all the bags into the valley and dumped by the clump of brambles, he then had to get them through the prickly bushes into the underground den. It was exhausting work and seemed to take ages. He was worried his Mum would miss him and come looking for him but when he stumbled, dirty, torn and sweaty into the kitchen, he saw that it had taken him less than an hour.

He was exhausted, and after changing his clothes, decided to spend the rest of the afternoon playing with Pip and her friend. They thought he was very funny and especially liked it when he lay on the floor pretending to be ill so they could play at being nurses and doctors with Pip's medical kit. In fact he was glad just to lie on the floor and rest after all his hard work. But even as the little girls giggled and fussed around him, at the back of his mind was the worry about all that money hidden in his drawer. He decided he would tell Mum about it at tea time before his Dad got home. He imagined her happiness when she realised she would be able to afford the furniture she wanted after all, and how grateful she would be to Tom.

When Paul came home from his friend's he nearly told him all about it, but decided to break the news to them both at the same time. Besides, Tom wasn't sure about his brother these days. Even though he was only three years older than Tom, he seemed so grown up and didn't seem interested in what Tom was doing any more. He always acted as though he was better than Tom and it sometimes made Tom wonder if his parents loved his brother more than him. After all he really was so much better than Tom at so many things. He was cleverer, tidier, funnier, kinder, better behaved and was more sensible, and Tom often felt he couldn't keep up with him.

His thoughts were interrupted by a scream from his Mum. Tom rushed into the kitchen to find her on the phone speaking to his Dad.

"How can that have happened?" he heard her say and then, "Who could have done it? Are you going to call the police? A thousand pounds is so much money." She was absolutely furious and Tom began to feel a bit sick. When she put the phone down she told him that someone had stolen a thousand pounds from their bank account. Seeing his worried face she told him that it would be ok and that the police would find the culprit.

"Don't worry your head, it's for me and Dad to sort out," she reassured him. Tom managed to nod and smile at his Mum before he rushed out of the kitchen to his bedroom. This was dreadful. It seemed that the money wasn't free after all. Someone had stolen it from his Dad, and that someone was him. The police would investigate and they would discover that he was the thief. Would they send him to prison? What would his parents think of having a robber son? Would they understand it was all a terrible mistake? He had only been trying to help but it had all gone terribly wrong. He had to get away before his Dad came home and the police came to ask questions and look around.

Chapter Nine: The Escape

Of course Tom knew where to go. Quickly he put on some warm clothes including his thick school coat. He crept downstairs and found the coast was clear. Mum, Paul and Pip were all talking in the sitting room. Going into the kitchen he grabbed a few bananas and apples from the fruit bowl and quietly let himself out of the back door. He hurried down the garden, over the hedge and was soon at the brambly entrance to his underground den. In his panic he hurriedly pushed through the prickly bushes, not caring that his hands and face were torn and scratched. Arriving at the bottom of the steps he flung himself on the dusty ground of his hideout and burst into bitter tears. Awful thoughts rushed through his head. What would his parents do when they found out? Would they ever forgive him? How long would he have to hide away in his den? Would the police hunt him down and find him here? Would his parents ever love him again? Would Paul definitely be their favourite son now?

Eventually his sobs died down and he realised that he had to be practical. First he went back up the steps and rearranged the bushes around the entrance so that no one could ever see it. Going back into the room he decided he may as well make himself comfortable. Switching on his torch he spread out his sleeping bag at the back of the room and arranged his spare clothes on the bench in one pile and the food and drink in another pile. He had to admit it looked quite cosy and he realised he could stay here for ages. During the day he would lie low but at night he could go into the valley and wander around. It was then he realised the one very important thing he had forgotten;

spare batteries for the torch. He quickly switched it off and sat on his sleeping bag in the pitch dark. He realised he could only switch the torch on when it was absolutely necessary and wondered how long the batteries would last.

Feeling around he found the bananas and ate two of them with some crackers, washed down with a few swigs of lemonade. Batteries weren't the only things he would have to ration and he wondered how long his food and drink would last him. As he sat there, his eyes gradually got used to the dark and he could see the grey shapes of the things around him. There was a faint gleam of daylight coming through the bramble entrance which made the room feel a lot less gloomy, but he would never be able to see well enough to read or write unless he had the torch on. He began to relax after the drama of the day; his eyes began to droop and curling up on his sleeping bag he nodded off. He didn't know how long he had been asleep but all of a sudden he was woken up by voices calling his name. It was his Mum and Dad:

"Tom, where are you? It's getting late; it's time you were home."

Looking up towards the entrance Tom saw that it had gone dark. He could hear the sounds of feet dragging through the undergrowth, past his hideout and towards the far corner of the valley. His parents were calling him all the time and then he heard his Dad shout,

"It's ok; I've found the tree house! I knew all that stuff he took would have to be somewhere! He'll be hiding in here." There was a pause and some crashing and banging and then his Dad's voice again,

"Oh no, he's not here; I was so sure he would be."

His Dad sounded worried and cross at the same time and he heard his Mum wail, "Where is he? We've looked everywhere, he's been gone ages."

"It's no good," he heard his Dad answer; "we'll have to call the police and report him missing."

Tom was horrified. Call the police? Report him missing? What should he do? He realised he could finish it all now by climbing out of his hiding place, apologise for worrying them and go back home with them. They would be cross with him for a while for running away and making them so anxious, they might even ground him for a bit, but it wouldn't be so bad. He was just about to climb up the steps and call to them when he remembered why he had run off. The money! They must have found it in his bedroom and thought he had stolen it. They weren't calling him because they were worried about him but they were looking for him because he was a thief and they were going to punish him. They weren't going to ring the police to ask them to find him but to arrest him for committing a crime.

With a sob he sank down at the bottom of the steps. He heard the two people he loved most in the world apart from Paul and Pip walking away from him, their voices growing fainter and fainter. Perhaps they would never love him again. His Dad would be so disappointed in him and so ashamed that his son was a thief and even worse, a thief who stole from his own parents.

Soon everything was quiet again. His parents must have gone back home to ring the police. Perhaps they would come looking for him the next day. He shuddered. He would have to stick it out and stay in his underground hideout until he could think of a better plan.

Creeping up the steps, he peered through the brambles and made sure no one was around. He crawled out through the bushes, wandered some way away and used a clump of grass as a toilet. Going back towards the hideout he looked up and saw that the dark sky was clear. A half-moon was trailing a path of light through the sky and hundreds of stars were gleaming in the darkness. He picked out some of the constellations his Dad had taught him and marvelled at the beauty above him. It made him feel very small and he wondered if anything up there cared about him or if he really was all alone.

He shivered and returned to the safety of his hideout. He thought he may as well go to bed, but first he tucked into a bag of crisps, some more crackers and a few gulps of the lemonade. He still felt very hungry but if he was going to make the food last he could only eat small portions. He thought of the lovely hot meal Mum would have prepared for the family at home, but it made him feel too hungry and sad. It was then he realised he had no money with him either, so there was no chance of him replenishing his stocks. How stupid of him. He could have bought more batteries too from the little supermarket near his house. But that would mean running the risk of being seen. No, he was better lying low and waiting for something to happen.

He climbed into his sleeping bag and tried to get comfortable but the ground was really hard and lumpy. As he lay there in the dark he suddenly realised with a blinding flash that he had done a really stupid thing. He'd run away to escape his parents' anger, but of course he was just putting off the moment he would have to face up to them. It would've been much better to stay and face the music from the start. After all they were his parents who loved him and would've sorted things out, but now he'd just made things even worse. With these gloomy thoughts running through his mind he wriggled around a bit more until he found a comfy position and before he knew it was fast asleep.

Chapter Ten: The Vanishing

He must have slept a long time because when he woke up he could see the bright light of the sun penetrating the brambles. The rays even shone onto the top two steps. He scrambled out of his sleeping bag and up the steps. Carefully he rearranged the brambles so that they made a thick wall of vegetation which no one could see through. Of course, it meant the sun couldn't see through either and now he was in virtual darkness again. He sat on his sleeping bag and ate one of the bread rolls, which had already gone hard; and some of the jam which he spooned out of the jar. He thought how easy it was to get up and ready. As he was wearing the same clothes as last night he didn't have to get dressed and there was nowhere to have a wash and clean his teeth. He licked his sticky fingers and wiped them on his top and thought,

"Now what am I going to do for the rest of the day? This is going to be a long, lonely day."

But he needn't have worried about being bored because almost immediately he heard the sound of voices approaching and the bark of dogs.

"Spread out," ordered a voice. "I want every inch of this place searched."

The sound of boots swishing through the grass and sticks hitting the bushes came nearer and nearer and seemed to surround him. Terrified, he crouched at the very back of the room and pulled his sleeping bag over him. Perhaps even if they found the entrance they wouldn't notice him hiding in the darkness. He could feel his heart beating fast and there was a thumping inside his head. The sounds got nearer and nearer and Tom was sure they would see the hole under the brambles. Someone even hit the bush with a stick but then moved on and the sounds gradually faded. He heard a shout and men running and he supposed they had found his empty tree house. He hoped they would think he had spent the night there and then moved on out of the valley when day light came. He was just about to heave a sigh of relief when he heard the men and dogs returning. Once again he heard his clump of brambles rattle and shake but once again the men passed by and moved on towards the hedge.

"Ok men, he seems to have vanished," shouted the same voice as before. "We'll move on to the park and playground and see if he's there."

Soon all he could hear was the chirping of a bird in one of the trees. Tom could hardly believe his luck. They hadn't found him! He realised he was holding his breath and crouching in a most uncomfortable position. He took a huge gasp of air and stood stiffly to his feet. He felt all shaky and putting his sleeping bag flat on the floor, he sat down heavily on it. At first he felt incredibly relieved – he was free, they hadn't caught him, he wasn't going to jail. But then a terrible darkness swept over him. What was he going to do? He could only really stay here until his food and drink ran out, perhaps a few more days. Then what would he do? The longer he stayed here, the angrier his parents would become and the harder it would be to go home and face them. He decided he would have to think of another plan and hoped an idea would come to him. But the more he racked his brains, the emptier his head became. He remembered his Dad once telling him that if you were trying to remember something, the best thing to do was stop thinking about it and all of a sudden it would pop into your head. Perhaps if he stopped thinking about it, he would suddenly have a great idea.

But thinking about his Dad made him feel sad and he realised he had really messed up. It had been bad enough having a secret tree house and underground den, but he had stolen things from home including quite a lot of food. Worse, he had stolen money from his Father, even though he had thought it was free, and had hidden it. Now he was causing his parents a lot of trouble by going missing. He remembered his Dad once saying that it cost a lot of money when people were rescued from house fires by firemen, or from sinking boats by the coastguards. He supposed it was costing a lot of money for all these police men and dogs to be out looking for him. The worst thing of all was imagining his Dad being really angry with him. Perhaps he would never forgive him. Perhaps he would never love him or like him again. That was such an awful thought that Tom couldn't bear it. He jumped up quickly and decided he would have to do something to keep himself busy. First he would have some breakfast and then he would creep out of his hiding place to see what was going on.

He ate the last of the rolls which were rock hard by now and some more jam from the jar. To be healthy he ate two apples and then took huge gulps of lemonade from the first bottle which was already now almost empty. That meant he now needed to visit his toilet bush so he pushed his way out through the brambles and carefully rearranged them in case someone came by.

After a trip to the bush, he decided to go and see what was happening at his house. Going down on all fours, he crawled through the grass and bushes, thankful he was wearing long sleeves and his woolly gloves. It seemed to take ages and by the time he got to the hedge, he was very hot and sweaty and covered in dust and leaves. The sun was beating down on his head and it made him feel quite sick. Peering over the hedge he looked into his back garden and towards the house. No one was around. No Mum hanging out the washing or busy in the kitchen. All the windows were shut and empty and there was no sound at all. No Pip chatting away in her high little voice and no Mum and Dad answering her. No sign of Paul either. The house was deserted and it felt as though they had abandoned him.

Chapter Eleven: Alone and Terrified

Slowly and painfully he crawled back through the valley and down the steps to the room he was now beginning to think of as his prison. There was nothing to do, and no other plan had sprung into his mind so he thought he may as well have an early lunch. He ate far more than he intended: the rest of the bananas and crackers, half a packet of chocolate biscuits and some cake. At this rate the food would soon be gone. He lay down heavily on his sleeping bag and as there was nothing to do and all was quiet, he soon drifted off to sleep.

When he awoke he realised it had gone dark and he couldn't believe he had slept so long. He decided to go back and check on the house just to make sure they hadn't really all gone away and left him. Taking his torch with him, he pushed his way out. The ground was very uneven and he stumbled clumsily along, not even bothering to crawl. His torch cast weird shadows on the trees and bushes and it all looked very eerie. If he hadn't known where he was he would have thought he was lost; it all looked so different and somehow frightening. He could hear little scuffling sounds from the bushes and once his torch shone on two bright little eyes. He nearly jumped out of his skin and let out a little shriek. The two eyes vanished and he realised it must have been a mouse or some other little creature.

When he got to the hedge he switched off his torch and looked towards his house. He was amazed. Every single window was lit up and there seemed to be hundreds of people moving backwards and forwards, silhouetted against the light. What were they all doing there? Were they having a party without him? How could they leave him out? Why would they wait to have a party until he wasn't there? Then he saw the back door open and light from the kitchen streamed into the garden. His Father came out and stood alone in the light. Tom could see that his shoulders drooped and his hair was a mess. He certainly wasn't wearing his party clothes; these were the ones he used for gardening or doing messy jobs around the house.

Suddenly Tom realised they weren't having a party at all. These were the people who had been looking for him all day and his Dad had obviously been searching in all sorts of dirty places. He had got himself really messy looking for him.

At that moment Dad lifted his head and called out, "Tom, Tom, where are you? Come back." His voice sounded funny: all rough and cracked. His Dad stood there as if he was listening for his son to answer – but Tom said nothing. After a while his Dad turned round and went slowly back into the house and shut the door. Tom couldn't see him anymore, the light had gone. Sobbing, Tom turned round and hurried back to the bramble bush as fast as he could. He realised he could hardly see through the tears which were streaming down his face.

As he neared the den, a large, dark shape moved in front of him and he heard a sort of snuffle and a grunt. The shape moved towards him and, terrified, Tom was just about to let out a loud scream when in the beam of the torch he caught a glimpse of black and white fur and a shiny black nose. The big badger shuffled past him into the bushes and at that moment, everything went black. The torch batteries had run out. In a panic, Tom threw himself into the clump of brambles, scrabbling to get inside his hideout as quickly as possible. He had taken off his gloves to switch the torch on and off more easily and now his hands and face got really badly scratched. At that moment he didn't even feel the pain. All he wanted to do was get inside and curl himself up in a ball. The badger had frightened him, but worse than that was the terrible sight of his Father, standing in the garden, desperately calling for his lost son.

Miserably Tom felt his way over to his sleeping bag and slumped down on it. After a while he became aware of the pain in his hands and face and felt something warm trickling down into his eyes and mouth. He was bleeding quite badly and he didn't even have a tissue to mop himself up with. In a funny way, Tom didn't mind. He felt that he somehow deserved this pain, as a sort of pay back for the pain he was causing his parents.

There was nothing else for it. Tom stretched out a hand and in the dark found the rest of the cake, the other half of the packet of biscuits, some more crisps and the pot of jam. He stuffed them all down quickly, hoping they would make him feel better but all it made him feel was rather sick. He decided that crisps and spoons full of jam didn't go very well together.

Getting into his sleeping bag, Tom hoped that by falling asleep he would be able to forget the mess he was in. He was just dropping off to sleep when there was a loud crashing in the bushes outside and then a most unearthly scream. The hairs stood up on the back of his neck. Whatever was going on? The noise came again, like a woman screaming as though she were being murdered. The bushes crashed again and the screams came again and again, echoing down into his room, over and over. Terrified, he crawled into the farthest corner of the room and covered his ears with his hands. He stared through the dark at the place where the entrance was, expecting something or someone to burst in at any moment. A few minutes passed and he was starting to relax when a sort of howl rang out and then the scream again, but this time a bit further away. Another few minutes and then came another scream and howl and a sort of barking just by the entrance. Tom imagined someone running up and down the valley, being chased by a howling creature or a beast or a monster, sometimes nearby and sometimes further away. It was obvious he was going to have to stay awake and on guard all night in case the someone or something crashed into his hideout and attacked him.

So all through the night, he crouched huddled in his sleeping bag, staring into the darkness. Once or twice he nodded off but the strange noises soon alerted him and he sat up, ears straining to hear the sound of approaching danger. Eventually the black hole of the entrance turned grey. Morning was coming and the strange sounds had disappeared with the darkness. Cold and stiff, dried blood caking his hands and face, he carefully poked his head through the undergrowth. He thought he would have to see if there were signs of a fight and injured or even dead bodies. He first visited his toilet bush and then as he looked around he saw that everything was just as it had been the day before and he began to feel a bit silly. What had he actually been afraid of; just strange noises in the dark? It was then he remembered a holiday in Wales when he was little where he had heard similar noises in the night. His Dad had told him it was foxes screaming and barking. Was that all it had been last night?

As he continued to look around, all that seemed different was the weather. It had grown a lot colder and the sunny blue skies of yesterday had grown cloudy and dark. They had not had rain for weeks and there was talk on the television of a drought and farmers not being able to water their crops. Tom's Dad had not had to cut the lawn for weeks and the grass had turned yellow and stubbly. He supposed they needed the rain but didn't fancy being out in it.

He shivered and went back down the steps. He put on another top and searched for any remaining food. There were two apples and a few crackers he had missed before. He ate hungrily and drank the last of the lemonade. Gosh, it really was cold. He put on a fleece and snuggled down in his sleeping bag to keep warm. He realised that no brilliant plan had leapt into his mind. All he could think of was how miserable, cold and hungry he felt, and how much he missed his family. As he had been awake all night, and as there was nothing else to do, he decided a sleep might make him feel better.

Chapter Twelve: The Deluge

He slept for several hours and when he woke up he saw through the brambles that although it was still day time, the light seemed a funny grey colour. He scrambled out to use the toilet bush and was astonished to see that the sky was dark grey and black. Huge clouds were piling up in big purple banks and a fierce cold wind was blowing. Tom thought of going to check up on his house and family, but had only gone a few metres when huge drops of rain started to plop down. At first just a few, but soon a torrent of water was pouring from the fierce looking sky.

Tom dashed back and hurried down the steps. As he reached the room there was a flash of lightning followed almost immediately by a crash of thunder. Rain fell more heavily and the wind gusted, blowing through the brambles. Tom threw himself onto his sleeping bag and watched and listened as the storm raged outside. He was glad of his cosy room and was even happier that at least he wasn't afraid of thunder and lightning like some children he knew. He might be frightened of weird noises in the night but storms held no terror for him.

The storm seemed to last for ages and the last light of the day was disappearing as the rain and wind eased up a bit. Tom was cold and put on his thick school coat which he was grateful to have brought with him. Now he was so bundled up with clothes he could hardly move but even so his feet were cold and he decided to wrap a remaining track suit top around them. As he stretched out his hand in the dark to reach it, he got a shock. The ground was wet. At first he thought it was just a small puddle, perhaps caused by a trickle of water coming through the roof. But as he moved his hand around him he realised he was surrounded by water at least two centimetres deep. Just then he noticed that his trousers were wet and that his sleeping bag was becoming soaked. He jumped up and took a few steps towards the entrance. The further he went from the sleeping bag, the deeper the water got and by the time he got to the bottom of the steps his trainers and the bottom of his jeans were soaking.

He heard it at the same time as he saw it. A waterfall was trickling down the steps from outside and even as he watched, the trickle turned into a small torrent and then into something like a mini Niagara Falls. Behind him he could see the dark water swirling as it started to creep up the sides of the walls. Soon he was wet up to his knees and still the water surged into his hideout. He waded to the ledge running round one side of the room and climbed onto it, tucking his feet and legs up out of the flood. But in only a few minutes the water was creeping over them again. He realised that the torrential rain must have caused a flood in the valley and now it was pouring into his den. Of course it hadn't rained for so long that any previous flooding had long since dried out and he'd had no idea that his place of safety could become a death trap. And that was what was happening. Looking down he could see biscuit wrappers and something which looked like one of his socks swishing round in the black water.

The waterfall coming down the steps showed no sign of slowing down and the water level was still rising. Soon his whole body would be under water and then his head. He would be trapped against the roof of his den, unable to breathe and then he would drown. He didn't panic but saw clearly what he must do. Not only did he have to escape up the steps to safety but he also had to go home. He wouldn't be able to stay outside, soaked through and freezing cold.

There was nothing for it but to admit defeat. His escape plan had failed and in a flash he saw that it could never have worked. Had he really thought that he could hide forever? Even more important did he really think that he wanted to hide from his family forever? Of course not! At home he had absolutely everything he needed, food, shelter, safety and love. Here he was, cold, miserable, frightened, and lonely and in great danger of drowning, when at home all was safe and bright and happy. There was nothing for it. He would have to go home and say he was sorry for stealing the money and running away. Hopefully in time, Dad would forgive him and all would be ok between them again.

All this went through Tom's mind in a flash. He knew he would have to hurry or he would never be going anywhere again! Sliding off the ledge, he slipped into the water. It was absolutely freezing and already half way up his chest. It completely took his breath away and he gasped, trying not to panic. He had to push against the water, taking small careful steps. If he slipped he would be under the water in no time and he really wasn't a very good swimmer. Slowly he waded towards the bottom step and looked up to the entrance. Water was still cascading down the steps. Taking a deep breath he slowly crawled up the stairs on his hands and knees, the water rushing over him and nearly dragging him back down. Once, when the boiler had broken at home, Tom had to have a cold shower, but it was nothing like this. The water was icy and black and it felt as though bucket after bucket of it was being poured over him. After what seemed like a life time he reached the top step and pushed through the brambles. By this time he was numb with cold and couldn't feel the thorns tearing at his hands and face. Stumbling to clear ground he found he could hardly stand up. The weight of the water in all his layers of clothes almost dragged him to the ground. He was shivering uncontrollably and could hardly put one step in front of the other. All the time he kept thinking about how angry his parents would be. He couldn't bear to think how they would punish him. Grounded forever? Only allowed out to go to school? Not allowed to join in the family's fun? Left out of everything? Tom wondered how anyone could feel so sad and miserable and still be alive.

Chapter Thirteen: The Homecoming

As slow as a slug, he crept across Fern Valley, dragging his tired legs through puddles, past the remains of the little garden which had been washed away, and up to the hedge. Pushing through, he was in his garden again and looking towards the house he saw that once again every light was on in every window. He shuffled up the garden towards the back door. In his head he rehearsed what he would say, "Dad, I'm sorry, I didn't mean to steal the money, I thought it was free."

He couldn't think any further than that and as he reached the door he dreaded what his family would say and do when they saw him. He was shivering so much he could hardly knock on the door and in the end it was a sort of thumping sound which his father heard. Dad flung open the door and saw standing outside in the dark his beloved son. His soaking, shivering son, dressed in layers of filthy clothes, whose hands and face were covered in scratches, fresh blood mixed with tears running down his cheeks. Tom tried to step up into the kitchen but didn't seem to have any strength left.

"I'm sorry Dad," he started to say but with a great whoop of joy, his Dad bent down and lifted him into the kitchen. Light flooded all around him. Tom realised that although he was filthy dirty and dripping streams of muddy water all over the floor, his father was hugging and kissing him as though he would never stop.

"Wherever have you been?" he asked Tom, "I've been searching for you everywhere. I thought you were lost forever."

51

Then he turned and shouted, "Quick, come here everyone, he's back, we've found him, we've found him!"

Suddenly the room was filled with his family; his Mum laughing tears of joy, Pip jumping up and down and squealing with excitement, all four of his Grandparents beaming and smiling, tears trickling down their cheeks. Tom realised they must have come to help find him. He was overwhelmed with warmth and happiness; he was back home. He realised that no one was cross with him or was telling him off. No one asked about the money or the things he had taken from the house. All they wanted to know was if he was alright, where had he been, how had he survived.

Suddenly his Dad shouted, "We'll have a celebration! I'll order all Tom's favourite food and we'll have a party to celebrate his return! But first, off with those soaking filthy clothes and go and have the longest, bubbliest hot bath you've ever had. There are new clothes for you in your bedroom. Come on, let's celebrate!"

Tom gazed up at his Dad. He could hardly believe it; it was going to be alright! Relief and happiness welled up inside him and it seemed he could hardly bear all the love poured out on him. But one thing worried him and taking off his trainers and coat, he shuffled into the hall. There was Paul, and Tom realised that his brother hadn't been in the kitchen to welcome him. In fact he looked cross and miserable and Tom thought that perhaps he wasn't as pleased to see him back as the others.

"Upstairs you go," Dad said to Tom following him into the hall. "Mum's running the bath for you and I've phoned for a takeaway."

Tom started upstairs and saw his Dad talking to Paul. He hugged him and said, "Don't sulk, Paul. Be happy your brother is back. I know he's caused all sorts of trouble - but he was lost and we've found him. You'll always be my first son and I'll always love you. Come on, let's set the table together and get everything ready for the best party ever." Paul only shrugged and went off reluctantly to help his Dad.

Tom enjoyed the best bath he could remember. He could hardly believe it! He was home and everything was going to be alright! Amazingly, it seemed he was already forgiven and he realised his safe return home was much more important to his parents than anything else. He saw that he had been right all along – his Dad really was the best in the world! Now he was free and could look forward to the rest of the summer, playing in the tree house in Fern Valley and sharing it with his friends. As for the underground den, he thought that was best forgotten about!

Can you tell that The Vanishing is a modern retelling of The Parable of the Lost Son?
Check out Luke 15 verses 11-32 in the Bible to see what you think.

The hidden meaning of this parable is that God loves you so much that whatever you have done, he is always waiting for you to turn to him to ask him to be the best father ever to you.

* Have you found God's love for you?

The Vortex

Chapter One: Fern Valley Ventures

"I can't believe we soon won't be able to play in the tree house," moaned Tom.

"I know," agreed Ali," who wants to go to school anyway?"

It was the last week of the summer holidays and Tom and Ali were not particularly looking forward to going back to school. They had enjoyed a fantastic few weeks playing in their tree house in Fern Valley and couldn't bear the thought of it all coming to an end.

"We can still come after school until it gets dark, and at the weekends," said Ali.

"But it won't be the same as being able to spend all day here," sighed Tom, "and it won't be as easy for the others to come along."

After an argument, Ali's holiday abroad and Tom's week spent grounded at home, the two boys had decided to invite their friends to play with them in Fern Valley. The twins, Jill and Jackie had joined them nearly every day. They were identical twins and very mischievous. When they'd been born, their parents had ambitiously called them Gillian and Jacqueline but had soon realised that Jill and Jackie was much simpler, and that's how everyone knew them. Nobody could tell them apart except their parents and they were always playing tricks on their friends so that they were never quite sure which twin had done what. When they weren't giggling and whispering together they were good fun and had great ideas for new games. The best one was pretending that the tree was an emergency helicopter, always flying into dangerous situations and rescuing people. They called themselves The Whirlybirds and their only disagreements were about who were going to be the heroes and who were going to need rescuing.

They were often joined by Jim who lived in the big house on the corner of their road. He was rather posh and a bit snooty but he seemed to want to join in and always brought lots of snacks to share. He was especially good at climbing high up into the tree so they often used him as the lookout to see if anyone was coming. If he saw someone he would give a shrill whistle and they would all clamber up into the house and hide until the intruders had gone.

Two rather timid girls called Laura and Amelia had joined them occasionally. Although they were rather afraid of the twins they loved the freedom of playing in Fern Valley and soon stopped minding that their clothes got messy and that they were covered in scratches and bruises. They had all spent hours and hours playing all sorts of games together and called themselves The Fern Valley Venturers.

None of them knew about the real adventure Tom had recently experienced, and none of them knew about the secret underground den he had found. The entrance had been covered with concrete for safety reasons and was hidden under brambles and weeds just a few metres away from the tree house.

"Let's have one last picnic tomorrow," suggested Tom. "We'll make it a really big one and afterwards we can tidy up the tree house and take anything valuable back home."

They all liked the idea of the picnic but no one much fancied tidying up.

"I'll ask Mum to make sandwiches," suggested Jim. "And I can bring some biscuits too."

"Mum is baking cakes today," said Jackie.

"Oh yes, I'm sure she'll let us have some," said Jill. "I hope she's made lemon drizzle cake, it's my favourite."

"I'll bring some drinks," offered Ali, "and perhaps you could bring fruit Tom."

"Oh yes," agreed Tom, "and some sweets and chocolate too."

Laura and Amelia volunteered popcorn and crisps and the children soon had a feast prepared.

Their last day together at the tree house felt quite sad. After a huge picnic and a last game of Whirlybirds they each gathered their toys and books, the torch, cushions and rugs and dragged them back through Fern Valley and to their homes. The tree house was left bare, empty and forlorn looking.

"Never mind, "they told each other, "there are always the weekends and we can all come back next summer and make the house even better."

And so the long summer holiday came to an end for the Fern Valley Venturers. Little did they know that they would all soon be involved in some rather more frightening adventures.

Chapter Two: New Beginnings and a New Arrival

"We have good news," announced Mrs Barton, Year Four class teacher at Fern Valley Primary School.

Ali pricked his ears up. He had been day dreaming about the summer holidays which were now over, and wishing that he was still playing in the treehouse in Fern Valley with his friends. It had been great fun being with them rather than by himself at home as he usually was in the holidays. Now it was all over and there were in year four in their new classroom, all wearing shiny, new, black school shoes and smart uniforms, ready for a new school year.

"A new family is coming to Fern Valley Primary. There are four children and one of them will be joining our class. His name is Sameer Rahim and he and his family have come from another country to live in England."

Tom breathed a sigh of relief. "Thank goodness it's a boy," he thought. "There are already too many girls in this class."

"Sameer's family have had a very difficult time in their own country and I want all of you to be especially kind and friendly," Mrs Barton continued. "The hardest thing is that he doesn't speak any English so it won't be easy to talk to him at first, but I know I can rely on all you to be helpful and make him feel at home."

Ali thought how awful it must be to have to leave your own country and come to another where you can't even understand what's going on. He decided he would help this new boy as much as he could.

"The family aren't arriving just yet so we will have time to get settled in ourselves first. So I want you all to get out your Literacy books and we'll start by writing about what you did during the summer."

Tom sighed, "Why did teachers always ask them to ruin the holidays by making them write about them?" he wondered. He got out his books and pen and was soon back to day dreaming about his Fern Valley tree house adventures.

A week had passed and all the children in Year Four had settled back into school life. Tom and Ali got on well together but they were a bit wary of Jill and Jackie the identical twins, both with ginger hair, freckles and mischievous grins. They seemed different now they were all back at school and you could never be sure if they were laughing at you or with you and Ali didn't know if they were being nice to him or making fun of him. He tried to steer clear of them, but either Jill or Jackie always seemed to be there, tripping him up or knocking his pencil onto the floor. Jim seemed to have changed too and was often moody and cross; so usually Ali and Tom played together every day and often included Laura and Amelia in their games.

The Rahim family were due to arrive in school the next day. Ali and his friends were eager to meet them and make friends with Sameer. They were shocked to hear some of the children complaining that their school was already too full and that they didn't need kids who couldn't even speak English coming into each of the junior classes. In particular Jim seemed determined that he wasn't going to make friends with the new boy.

"I'm not going to play with any foreigners," he said. "They should stay in their own countries and not come bothering us here."

Tom and Ali couldn't believe what Jim had said. They had enjoyed playing with him in the tree house, but since they were back at school Jim seemed to have changed. He had become rude and unfriendly and didn't seem to want to play with them anymore. They didn't know if they should tell Mrs Barton what he had said but didn't really want to get him into trouble.

There was a rumour that Sameer had two other sisters who were still too young to go to school. Ali did think that six children was a big family, but it would probably be good fun. Only having a little sister, he was always wishing he had brothers to play with.

Jim had other ideas, "Six kids!" he said. "Imagine how much that is going to cost the government to feed and educate them all!"

Tom and Ali were glad that Jim had been whispering. They couldn't bear to think other children had heard the awful things he was saying and hoped that he would keep his thoughts to himself. They thought that perhaps they didn't want to be friends with Jim anymore.

Mrs Barton asked Tom and Ali to be buddies with Sameer for the first week. It would be their job to show him around and make sure he didn't get lost and to play with him so he didn't feel lonely.

At last the new boy arrived in the class room, ushered in by the Head teacher and greeted by Mrs Barton. Sameer was tall and thin and Ali noticed that his uniform was too small for him. It was obviously second hand and it was a shame they couldn't have found him something that fitted better. He looked very nervous, his big eyes stared round at all the children looking at him, and a sad little smile was on his lips. He was shown to the table where Ali and his friends were sitting and they all smiled at him. He sat down and Ali noticed there were tears in the corners of his eyes. It was a numeracy lesson and it soon became obvious that Sameer really didn't understand any English at all. Mrs Barton said that sometimes there would be a teaching assistant to help explain things to him but not today.

Playtime wasn't much better as they tried their best to make Sameer feel at home. They shared their snacks with him and got him to play football with them. They showed him where the toilets were and where they would go to eat lunch. But really all he was interested in was finding his brothers and sisters and standing in a huddle with them, whispering to them in a language no one else could understand.

"This is going to be harder than I thought," Ali said to Tom. They both agreed they would have to work hard to make Sameer feel happy and to teach him some English.

"It must be awful not to understand a word of what's going on," said Ali. "No wonder they just want to talk to each other."

Tom agreed, "New country, new house, new school, new people, new language. Of course they want to stick together."

Chapter Three: Settling In

The weeks passed and soon Sameer was one of them. It was amazing how quickly he learnt enough English to be able to play with his new friends. School work was harder, but it soon became obvious that he was a very clever boy as he started to do better in some of their weekly mini tests than some of the others in the class.

Ali said it wasn't surprising he was clever as he had heard that Mr Rahim had been a doctor before he brought his family to England.

"But why does he just work in the little corner shop if he is a doctor?" asked Tom.

Just then Jim slouched up and sneered, "He probably isn't a proper doctor. I don't suppose they have any real doctors from where they come from," he laughed. "He's probably made it all up."

"I think it will be because he doesn't speak good English yet," said Ali, scowling at Jim. "Once his English is good enough, I'm sure he will be able to work in a hospital here."

The friends were really getting fed up with Jim and his nasty comments about Sameer, and that wasn't their only problem. The twins had been getting up to mischief and making Mrs Barton cross. As she couldn't tell them apart, she had asked them to have their hair in different styles from each other and wear different coloured hair clips. Each day the girls had arrived at school looking exactly the same as each other apart from their hair. They had each sat in their own places and Mrs Barton knew who was who, but by the time morning break was over, they had changed their hair to look exactly the same as each other. Sometimes they sat in their proper places but every now and again they swapped seats and pretended to be each other.

"Now Jackie, can you tell us what we were doing in science last week?" asked Mrs Barton.

"I'm not Jackie," giggled the girl, "I'm Jill."

Even most of the children weren't sure who was who. If one of the twins slyly pinched them or tripped them up they would complain to Mrs Barton.

"Mrs Barton, Jackie just tripped me up."

"Jackie, why did you trip Jacob up? Apologise immediately."

"But it wasn't me, it must have been Jill."

"No it wasn't me, it was you," Jill said.

The girls giggled and smiled at each other, they so enjoyed confusing everybody and sometimes it was really quite funny. But Mrs Barton didn't think so and she was becoming quite bad tempered. So one day, when she overheard Jim say something rude about Sameer and his family she blew up.

"Jim Brown, how dare you talk like that about someone behind his back?" she yelled. "I will NOT put up with anything like that in my classroom. We are happy to welcome a newcomer into our class wherever they come from and whoever they are. Don't let me ever hear you or anyone else say anything like that again or you will be off to the Headmaster before you can turn round. Do you understand?"

"Yes Mrs Barton," Jim answered, a little smile flickering round his lips as he spoke.

"Now go and apologise to Sameer at once and remember I will be watching you from now on."

Jim said he was sorry to Sameer, but he didn't look very sorry. From then on he kept his thoughts to himself but Ali and his friends knew that for some reason he seemed to hate Sameer and his family.

Tom, Ali, Laura and Amelia made an extra special effort to be nice to Sameer and mostly they all got on really well but sometimes they caught Sameer looking sad. He seemed lost in thought and the children wondered if he was thinking about his old home and wishing he was back there.

Chapter Four: Going on an Adventure

It was Friday, a few weeks into the term and the class was preparing to go home for the weekend.

"Listen carefully, children. As you know, our class is due to go to Princefield Adventure Centre for four days in October," said Mrs Barton. "Before you all go, I am going to give you the details for you to take home to your parents and we will be going in two weeks time!"

The class erupted into excited chatter.

"Here is a list of all the clothes and equipment you will need and an acceptance form for your parents to fill in. As you know, this is an expensive trip and those parents who will find it hard to pay will be helped from our school holiday fund, so everyone will be able to go."

"Huh, "whispered Jim, "that's a shame. I hoped Sameer would be too poor to afford to come. But I suppose I will have to put up with him for four whole days and nights."

Ali and Tom, who were sitting next to Jim gasped in horror and quickly looked to see if Mrs Barton had heard Jim. But the noise from the excited children had drowned out Jim's cruel words and Mrs Barton continued:

"Bring your form and payment back as quickly as possible, and start to get your clothes and equipment ready this weekend."

Mrs Barton seemed almost as excited as the children at the prospect of almost a week away from school. Perhaps if she had known just what was in store for them all, she might not have been so keen to spend four days and nights with Year Four!

Princefield Activity Camp was about fifty miles away and deep in the countryside. The children had already heard all sorts of stories about what went on at the centre. There were tales of jumping off high towers with only a harness to keep you safe, wading waist deep in a cold river, mud fights, night walks in the dark and other rather scary activities. They had heard they were going there to build their confidence and courage and to help each other by working in teams. Secretly, some of the class felt really nervous about this time away. For many it would be the longest they had ever stayed away from home and the thought of sleeping in wooden huts at night and doing all sorts of daring things during the day was not their idea of fun. Of course, no one dared to voice their fears and everyone put on a brave face whatever they were feeling.

"This is going to be great," Jackie giggled, "we'll be able to play all sorts of tricks on people without getting found out."

"I know," replied Jill, we're going to have so much fun."

"Of course I've already been to a camp like this," boasted Jim, "I'm really good at all this stuff, just you wait and see."

"I hope I'm in your hut and on the same teams as you," Laura said anxiously to Amelia.

"Don't worry, we'll stay together and stick up for each other," Amelia reassured her. "We'll be ok."

Ali sat alone and quiet, surrounded by his excited class mates. He wasn't looking forward to the time away and it made it worse that everyone else seemed so keen on going. As he looked round the room, he spotted one other person who looked as though he was feeling the same way. Sameer was sitting by himself, his face a picture of misery and confusion.

"Of course," thought Ali, "he doesn't have a clue what all this is about and will never have been away on a camp like this. No wonder he looks so worried."

"That's enough now children," Mrs Barton raised her voice. "It's home time now. Make sure you take your kit list and acceptance form home with you for your parents. Now let me see who is ready to go home first."

Chapter Five: A Dreadful Incident

That weekend Ali thought of telling his parents that he didn't want to go on the camp. But they were thrilled that he was going away with his friends and didn't seem to have any idea about his fears.

"What a wonderful opportunity dear," his mother said. "How lovely to spend all that time with your friends doing all those exciting things. I never did anything like this when I was your age. We must go out and buy all your equipment."

Ali didn't have the heart to tell her how he was really feeling and with a sinking heart went with her on the shopping expedition. They bought a sleeping bag, a sturdy torch, a pair of wellington boots and a thin waterproof coat. They already had everything else on the list. Ali wondered why on earth he would need a set of old clothes that could be thrown away. What was he going to be doing that would ruin a set of clothes? He wondered why he would need a warm coat, scarf, gloves and woolly hat. It was only October, not the middle of winter. Why did he need lots of T shirts and shorts that he could get wet in but no swimming trunks? The more they gathered together the things on the list, the more excited his mother got and the more worried he became.

"I think your Dad's big holdall should be big enough for all this," his Mum said. "What fun you're going to have!"

"I'm not sure I want to go," he stammered, but seeing his Mum's surprised face he added, "but I suppose it will be ok."

"Of course it will," his mother said cheerfully, "now I must put your name on all these things, we don't want them getting lost. Why don't you go to Fern Valley to see if any of your little friends are there?"

Ali decided to go to the tree house and hoped that some of the others would be there to play with. But as he walked through the valley towards the tree house he could hear raised voices.

It was Tom shrieking, "Whatever are you doing? Leave it alone!"

"It's only a babyish tree house, it's silly," somebody answered.

Ali was horrified to see the twins in the tree house, ripping down the walls and stabbing holes in the floor with sharp poles whilst Jim looked on, laughing. Tom, Laura and Amelia were standing helplessly below watching as their beloved house was destroyed.

He rushed forward, "What are you doing?" he shouted. "It took us ages to build it, leave it alone."

"And what are you going to do about it?" smirked Jim.

Ali didn't know what to do about it. He couldn't believe that Jill and Jackie wanted to wreck the place they had enjoyed playing in all summer. Then as he looked more closely at the girls, he saw that they were not enjoying what they were doing; in fact he saw that tears were streaming down their faces.

"Jackie, Jill, what are you doing?" he called out. "Why are you wrecking the tree house?"

"It was a dare," one of the twins answered quietly.

"What do you mean by a dare?" he asked.

"Well Jim dared us to do something naughty at school. We said we would do it because we thought it would be fun to annoy Mrs Barton, but that was before we knew what he wanted us to do," answered Jill.

"So we didn't do it and Jim said that as we hadn't completed the dare, we would have to destroy the tree house," answered the other girl. "We're really sorry."

The boys turned to look at Jim who had a very unpleasant smile on his face.

Ali and Tom spoke together, "What did you ask Jill and Jackie to do?"

"It was so easy," said Jim, "I can't think why on earth they wouldn't do it. I only asked them to take that boy Sameer's bag and throw it in the big rubbish bin on the street outside school. It would have been such fun to watch him look for it everywhere."

"Why are you so mean to Sameer? He's really nice, why do you want to make him miserable?" Ali asked between clenched teeth. He could feel himself getting really angry and he could hardly look Jim in the face.

"Well if he's really miserable, perhaps he'll go back to where he came from, him and all his horrible family."

As one, the two boys made a dash towards Jim. They wanted to get their hands on him and hit that horrible, smiling face. But as quick as a flash Jim was off, running out of the valley. When he was out of reach he turned round to face them.

"And don't any of you dare to tell anyone," he threatened, "or else."

With that he made his way out of the valley, walking slowly and confidently, his hands in his pockets and a tuneless whistle on his lips.

Jackie and Jill scrambled down the ladder to the boys. They all stood in silence, shocked and angry.

Eventually Jackie said, "We'll put the walls back up and I don't think we've damaged the floor too much."

"Yes," added Jill, "we'll be able to play here again, won't we?"

"No," said Tom, "just leave it as it is. I don't think I want to play here anymore. It's all spoilt."

"I agree," Ali muttered, "it will never be the same again. Perhaps we'll feel different after a while but at the moment I haven't the heart to rebuild it."

Both the girls burst into loud sobs, "We're really sorry," they spluttered.

"We had no idea what Jim was going to ask us to do," explained Jill.

"And of course we couldn't do that to Sameer, it would have been so mean," added Jackie.

"Well I'm getting fed up with your stupid tricks," said Tom. "They just aren't funny anymore."

"Yes, all you do is get Mrs Barton into a bad temper and then she shouts at all of us," complained Ali. "I think you should learn a lesson from this and stop fooling about so much."

Laura and Amelia nodded their heads in agreement.

"Ok, you're right," the twins said. "We'll try to be sensible from now on."

Everybody smiled and agreed and decided it was time to go back to their homes for tea, their mothers would be wondering where they were. Only Ali seemed to doubt the girls' promise, and only he seemed to be worried about Jim. What were they going to do with him? He seemed to be getting worse and worse and Ali couldn't understand why he seemed to hate Sameer so much.

"Oh dear," he thought," This week away on camp is going to be even harder than I first thought. I'm dreading it."

Little did he know how right he was to be worried.

Chapter Six: Princefield Activity Camp

The day had arrived at last. The children were all gathered outside school waiting for the bus to take them to Princefield Activity Camp. They each had a big bag stuffed full of the clothes and equipment they would need for their time away. Ali looked around and realised that his bag seemed bigger than everyone else's.

"Whatever have you got in that bag? You look as though you're taking everything but the kitchen sink!" someone laughed.

Ali's face went red and he wished he hadn't let his Mum put in all those "extra clothes in case you get cold," as she put it. She had also insisted on buying the biggest, fluffiest sleeping bag she could find and it took up a huge amount of space.

"Bother," he thought, "why do I always feel the odd one out?"

But then he looked over to the edge of the group and saw Sameer standing talking quietly to Tom. Lots of people had helped him out with clothes and equipment but it was obvious that no one had lent him a bag to put it all in. His possessions were stuffed into four plastic bags and Ali could see socks and trousers spilling out of the top of one of them. Ali felt ashamed and realised how lucky he was to be going on this trip at all. Sameer had told them that he had never been on holiday before because it was too dangerous to travel in his country and sometimes there hadn't even been enough money to buy food for them all. It had taken his father several years to save up enough money to pay someone to get them out of their country and eventually to England. They had arrived with little more than the clothes they stood up in. The boys had asked him several times how they had got to England, but Sameer's face always went all crumpled as if he was going to cry and told them he didn't want to say.

"And here am I moaning that I have got too much," thought Ali, "when his family came with nothing." He picked up his bag and wandered over to his friends who greeted him excitedly.

"This is going to be such fun," Ali said.

"I know," replied Sameer, "I hope they put us together in the same dormitory."

"Well they asked us who we wanted to be with so I am sure they will," Ali said. "I just don't know who will be in with us."

"Yes," said Tom, "there are only three of us and each dorm has six beds so we will just have to wait and see."

At that moment there was a cheer as the bus pulled onto the drive and everyone picked up their bags. In no time at all the bus was swishing out of the drive and everyone was waving goodbye to their parents.

"Ok, settle down and make sure your seat belts are fastened; we should be there in about an hour, so enjoy the journey," Mrs Barton said cheerfully.

At first there was a lot of chattering but as the bus took them out of their familiar surroundings the children quietened down and enjoyed looking out of the windows as streets and houses and then fields and trees rushed by. It did indeed take them just over an hour to reach Princefield which really was right in the middle of nowhere. Getting off the bus the children gazed round at trees and more trees, fields and more fields. In the distance there was the glimmer of sun on water. The only noise they could hear was birds in the trees and the distant shouts of children.

"Welcome!" boomed a man's voice. The children spun round to see two smiling people standing in front of the reception building.

"Welcome to Princefield," said the man, "my name is Bruce. We hope you are going to have a great time here. At Princefield the most important thing is that each one of you works hard, has a go at everything and does the best they can. We don't mind how good or bad you are at anything as long as you have a go. This morning we will show you round the camp and let you see the activities you will be involved in and then we'll have lunch."

"But first, let's assign you your dormitories and get you settled in," the woman said. Her name was Anne and she and Bruce were to be their leaders throughout the week. The children listened carefully as their names were read out. The three boys were very happy to hear they were all in Barn Owl Dormitory together with two boys called Arthur and Philip; but they all groaned inwardly when they heard the sixth name read out – Jim Brown.

"Why have they put him with us?" muttered Tom. "Surely they know that Jim hates Sameer."

"We'll just have to make the most of it," whispered Ali, "perhaps Jim will change his mind when he gets to know Sameer better."

"Yes, after all, we're not at school, it might be different here," Ali said hopefully.

Sameer just smiled but looked worried as Jim sidled up to them.

"Oh good, I'm with you lot, "said Jim, "it's going to be fun. Come on let's find this Barn Owl Dorm." As he walked away he gave one of Sameer's plastic bags a sharp kick and a bundle of socks and underpants spilled out onto the ground much to Sameer's embarrassment.

"Oh sorry Sameer," smirked Jim, "you really need to get a proper bag. Come on then everybody, what are you all waiting for?"

Once Sameer had stuffed his underwear back in the bag, the boys followed slowly behind Jim, all of them wondering how the week was going to turn out. They would just have to make the best of it and not let Jim spoil their time away.

Chapter Seven: Let the Activity Begin!

They found Barn Owl Dormitory, chose their bunks and unpacked. Their five dormitory huts were arranged together in a rough circle near the shower block and toilets. Laura and Amelia were with Jackie and Jill in Snowy Owl Dormitory next to the boys' hut, and as they unpacked, they could hear giggles and shrieks of laughter coming from the girls' hut.

Jackie and Jill had turned up in exactly the same track suits as each other, their hair in the same style and hair clips the same colour. You really couldn't tell them apart and Ali suspected that they were going to get up to as much mischief as possible and confuse the camp leaders whenever they could. Half of him thought it would all be quite funny, but the other half felt sorry for Amelia and Laura. They were still a little afraid of the twins and usually tried to avoid them but now they would be thrown together for four days and nights. The teachers had their own hut nearby and they were all about a five minute walk away from the reception building which housed the dining room, a large hall and smaller class rooms.

Once they had looked round the buildings, the leaders led them round the outdoor activity areas. First they went down to the lake where they would do water sports. Kayaks and rowing boats were lying in neat rows on the shore and next to them was a shed containing the life jackets.

"One of the most important rules at Princefield is that absolutely no one should ever go out on the water without a life jacket on," said Bruce. "The water may look calm, and it's not very deep, but anyone can drown in a tea cup. Besides that, over there, beyond the red buoys, where you can see those weeds in the water and the trees overhanging, is where the lake flows out into a little river. The water starts to move fast there and just round the corner there is a whirlpool and a series of small waterfalls and weirs. No one must ever go past those red buoys because if they do they will get caught in the whirlpool and be carried over the waterfalls. Your boat or kayak will almost certainly capsize and you would be thrown into rough, fast flowing water. Does everyone understand – no going past the red buoys?"

"Yes," the children chorused. It all sounded rather dangerous but also exciting at the same time.

Next they went into the woods where a lot of their activities would take place.

"Here you will work in teams and learn how to build shelters and make fires and how to find your way round in the dark," said Anne. "Over there are zip wires, bungee jumping towers and assault courses. You will each get the chance to challenge yourself to do your personal best and to help and encourage each other."

The children stared in astonishment at the high wooden towers and wires peeping through the trees. Some of them felt excited about the challenges they would be facing, but others felt nervous and scared.

Knowing how they must be feeling, Anne continued, "Don't worry, no one will be made to do anything they really don't want to do, but we will encourage you to overcome your fears and have a go. Of course, the most important rule here is that no one should ever go on any of the high equipment without the proper harnesses on, and no one should climb on anything without us being there to supervise you. Just as with the rules about the water sports, anyone breaking these rules will miss out on the day's activities. Understood?"

"Yes," the children chorused once again. By this time, some of them were wondering if the week was going to be one long terrifying ordeal but most of them were keen to get started on the adventures.

In the field were picnic tables, remains of camp fires and buildings housing all sorts of games' equipment.

"Here we will do team games and challenges," said Bruce, "and one night we will have a bonfire and sing songs and toast marshmallows."

"And now it's time for lunch, over in the dining room," said Anne. After you've eaten I will give you each the week's timetable and you can all read it and have a short rest before our first activity - bouldering!"

The children all headed to the dining room, chattering excitedly.

"I can't wait to have a go on the zip wire," said Tom.

"Neither can I," replied Ali, "and the bungee jumping looks awesome."

Laura and Amelia agreed they were most looking forward to the water sports.

"I wonder what bouldering is?" said Sameer. None of them knew.

Only Jim looked miserable. "How boring and babyish," he yawned. "I've done all this stuff before. Who wants to splash around in boats and crash around the woods in the dark? And I can see no fun in jumping off a tower into mid-air with only a rope to save you. What a bore!"

"Well you may as well enjoy it now you're here," Jill said cheerfully, "you can show us all how it's done."

But Jim only sniffed and walked off, his hands in his pockets and his head down. As he walked in front of Sameer, he suddenly stopped and bent down, fiddling with a shoelace. Sameer, who was talking excitedly to Tom, didn't see him and fell right over him, landing in a dusty heap on the ground.

"Watch where you're going," snarled Jim to the startled Sameer. A nasty little smile played round his lips and all the children knew that Jim had deliberately tripped Sameer up. They pulled Sameer to his feet and dusted him down, but no one said anything to Jim, not wanting to make things worse.

As they approached the dining room, a delicious smell wafted out, and the incident was soon forgotten as they tucked into a tasty lunch.

Chapter Eight: Bouldering!

After lunch Anne gave them the week's timetable of activities. The children were amazed at how much they were going to pack into each day. There were several different challenges every day before the evening meal and one night time activity too.

"Gosh," squeaked Jill," breakfast is at 8 o'clock, there will be no lie-ins for us!"

"What?" growled Jim, "I don't think I'll be getting up that early!"

"That's ok mate," laughed Bruce. "If you want to miss breakfast that's alright by us; but everyone has to tidy up and be ready for the first activity by 9.30."

"Sounds more like a labour camp than an activity camp to me," moaned Jim.

"Don't be so miserable!" laughed Jackie. "This is going to be such fun!"

"Yes," agreed Jill. "Come on everyone; let's find out what bouldering is all about."

Bruce led them all to a brightly painted wall with all sorts of different shaped bumps in varying colours going up the wall to the top. The bumps were hand holds and foot rests and the idea was to use them to climb to the top of the wall. As the wall wasn't too high and the climb looked quite easy, the children didn't have to wear safety harnesses. At first they each had several goes at getting to the top. Some children found it really hard to do at the beginning. One boy got stuck half way up and had to be helped by Bruce. One of the girls burst into tears before she had even started and said she was too frightened. But with a lot of help and encouragement soon all the children could climb the wall. Then they were split up into their dormitory teams and raced against each other's teams. The Barn Owl team realised they were very lucky to have Sameer with them. He moved gracefully and confidently up the wall and was easily the fastest in the class.

"Well done!" called Bruce, "You're a natural!"

Tom, Ali, Philip and Arthur watched in thrilled amazement as Sameer swarmed up the wall at great speed and then they took it turns to follow him. Jim was the last one up and everyone was surprised to see how slowly and carefully he moved. Although they had been one of the winning teams, by the time Jim reached the top they were second to last.

"Stupid game, "muttered Jim. He looked really miserable and the boys realised he wasn't as good at these activities as he had boasted before.

"Now," called out Bruce, "I want each team to climb the wall again but in a different order." So this time, Jim went first and Sameer was last. Once again Jim was slow and once again Sameer was very fast. The Barn Owl team cheered him on as he overtook other children and was soon at the top of the wall. But just as he put his hand on the top of the wall, Jim stepped forward and stamped on it. Sameer let out a yelp but despite his pain, managed to keep hanging on. The others rushed forward and pulled him up to safety.

"You stupid fool," yelled Arthur who was normally quiet and gentle. "He could have fallen right down to the bottom and really hurt himself." It was the first time Arthur had seen Jim's nasty behaviour to Sameer and he was shocked.

"We'll have to tell the leaders," he said. "Jim can't get away with that."

"No," said Ali and Tom together, "it will just make things worse."

"Yeah," grinned Jim, "what can you do about it?"

Just at that moment they all heard loud sobs and Mrs Barton shouting.

"I have told you girls not to get up to your tricks here," she scolded Jackie and Jill who were both crying. "What were you doing?"

"Jill is scared of heights so she didn't climb the wall and hid behind those bushes," Jackie explained. So I had to climb when it was my turn, then climb back down and climb up again pretending to be Jill. But I was going down so fast that I slipped and landed on someone going up. I'm sorry Amelia."

It was then they noticed Amelia sitting on the ground holding a towel to her head, blood seeping through it.

"I am ashamed of you," said Mrs Barton. "I thought my class would behave better than this."

"It's a good job she doesn't know what happened up here," thought Ali. "Then she really would be ashamed."

"Well," said Bruce, "As you have broken the safety rules and behaved badly, I am afraid you two girls will not be allowed to take part in any more activities until tomorrow. You will stay in one of the classrooms and do some written work."

The girls burst out crying again but were sent immediately to one of the classrooms.

"Ok," said Anne, "I hope that will be a lesson to you all. Breaking the rules and behaving badly will be punished immediately. Now come on everybody, cheer up, our next activity is Laser Quest. Follow me!"

The next hour was spent running around the woods, hiding behind trees, trying to shoot the enemy team and trying not to get shot themselves. It was great fun and even Amelia joined in after she had recovered.

The Barn Owl team discovered that none of them was a very good shot and they ended up losing. They didn't really mind and were relieved that Jim and Sameer seemed to enjoy playing together.

"Perhaps it's going to be ok," Ali whispered to Tom.

"I hope you're right," replied Tom, "but I wouldn't be too sure: you really can't trust Jim."

Chapter Nine: The First Night

After a delicious evening meal, the final activity before bed was a scrap heap challenge. Each team was given a pile of scrap and rubbish and was challenged to make something from it all. A leader was chosen for each team and the others had to follow their instructions. Everybody had a great time and all sorts of hilarious models were made.

At last it was bedtime and after a hot drink and a visit to the bathroom block, the children settled down into their dormitories. In Barn Owl Dorm Tom and Philip shared one bunk, Sameer and Ali another and Arthur and Jim the third.

"We've got fifteen minutes before lights out," said Tom. "Let's all get into bed and read before we go to sleep."

"Oh no, let's tell each other frightening stories," giggled Arthur as he snuggled into his sleeping bag.

Ali preferred the idea of reading and was just about to say so when he let out a scream. There was something cold and wet and slimy in his sleeping bag and he leapt out of bed onto the floor. Peering into the bag he realised it was just a clump of green, wet water weeds but it had soaked his sleeping bag and ruincd it.

"Who put this in my bed?" he yelled at the startled boys, although he was pretty sure who it had been.

Just then Jim drawled, "Oh, I'm sorry Ali. I thought you were going to sleep in the top bunk. That little present was meant for

Sameer not you. Perhaps Sameer will lend you his sleeping bag. You won't mind sleeping without covers, will you Sameer? You're probably used to it where you come from."

Without warning, and with a low growl, Sameer leapt out of his top bunk and dragged Jim and his sleeping bag out of bed and on to the floor. He yanked and pulled the sleeping bag until Jim was lying on the floor in his pyjamas.

"Here you are, Ali, you can have Jim's bag for the night," he said, thrusting it into Ali's startled arms. "Jim's the one who is going to do without any bed clothes tonight, unless you want the wet bag of course?"

Just at that moment there was a call of "Lights out! Sleep well!" and their hut was plunged into darkness. Everybody froze and then there was a series of scuffles as Sameer climbed back up to his top bunk, Ali crawled into Jim's sleeping bag below Sameer, and Jim got into his bed below Arthur, with or without the wet sleeping bag, no one knew. Everyone was stunned into silence and no one so much as said, "Good night". They all lay there shocked and miserable, far from sleep. The only sounds were some muffled sniffs and sobs from one of the boys and Ali was sure it was coming from Jim's bed.

"Serves him right," he thought. "I hope he has a miserable, wet, cold night."

Gradually, one by one, the boys fell asleep. Only Jim lay wide awake, miserable and cold. As he stared into the darkness, he wondered what had got into him. Why did he hate Sameer so much?

87

He felt as though he was being sucked into a whirlpool of hatred which he couldn't get out of. It was if he couldn't help being nasty to Sameer and he wondered where it would end.

Suddenly he heard a faint knocking at the door and someone whispering, "Open up."

Before he had time to decide what to do he heard an adult's voice shouting, "Who's that? Who's out of their dormitory? I am counting to ten and if I see anyone outside they will be sent straight back home tomorrow morning."

There was some scuffling and then silence until the same voice called again, "I expect everyone to stay in their beds now and go to sleep. We have a long and busy day ahead of us tomorrow."

Then there was complete quiet and eventually even Jim drifted off to sleep.

Chapter Ten: Challenges and Successes

A bell rang at seven o'clock next morning and everyone rolled out of bed, got washed and dressed and was ready for breakfast at eight o'clock. Only Jim muttered and turned over in bed when Tom tried to wake him. Rather relieved, the boys left him and hurried off to breakfast.

"Today, as you can see from the timetable, we are spending the morning on the zip wire and then abseiling down the towers," announced Bruce after breakfast. You have half an hour to get yourselves ready, tidy your dorms for inspection and then be back here ready to set off together into the woods."

"Oh no, "said Laura to Amelia, "I don't like the sound of either of these activities."

"I agree," replied Amelia. "For both of them you have to climb so high first, and I really don't like heights."

"Let's stick together and help each other," suggested Laura, and Amelia agreed.

"I hope Jim stays in bed all day," Tom said to Ali. "I can't believe he's being so horrible to Sameer."

"Yes, you can't trust him at all," agreed Ali, "but I expect he'll be joining in, he hasn't got any choice anyway."

Sure enough Jim was up and dressed and munching on a chocolate bar. "This is my breakfast," he said. "Just as good, and it gave me an extra hour in bed."

No one said anything about the night before, though they did notice that Ali's sleeping bag had been cleaned and was hanging up to dry. Together they trooped down to the meeting place and walked into the woods to the zip wire. Much to their amazement Ali and Arthur thoroughly enjoyed the zip wire and found they were really rather good at it. They could both travel further along the wire than many of the other children and won lots of points, making theirs the winning team. As they had come to expect, Sameer was fast and fearless and made it look so easy. The same was true for the abseiling. Ali and Arthur did better than they had expected and Sameer was the star once again.

"Well done Team Barn Owl," smiled Anne, the leader, "you should be proud of yourselves."

"Yes," Tom and Ali said to Sameer," you've done really well. We're so glad you are on our team!"

Only Jim looked as though he wasn't enjoying himself. "But at least he's behaving," the other boys thought to themselves.

To everyone's amazement, Laura and Amelia from the twins' hut had been made to stay in the classrooms for the morning. Apparently it had been they who were creeping around outside the dormitories the night before, knocking on doors. No one could believe they could be so naughty and everyone thought that the twins were probably behind it.

"Oh yes," giggled Jackie, "we dared them to go out and knock on doors and the silly girls did it."

"It was so funny," agreed Jill, "they've never done anything naughty in their lives before."

Today the twins were dressed in different clothes and it was easy to tell them apart. They had been allowed back to join in the activities and had been having great fun, leaving Amelia and Laura to take the punishment. In a way they were rather relieved as they hadn't been looking forward to the scary activities.

"After lunch we're raft building all afternoon," announced Bruce. Make sure you're wearing clothes and shoes you don't mind getting wet; and let's all meet by the lake at 1.30."

After a delicious hot lunch and a change of clothes, all the children went down to the water's edge.

There were plastic barrels, ropes, pieces of wood and other materials laid out on the shore.

"Now kids, this is a team challenge," said Anne. "You have to work together to design and make a raft from these materials. When you've built it, you have to try it out. Everyone in your team must sit on your raft and paddle it over to those blue buoys and back. Once we know your craft is sea worthy, then we will have races to see which team and raft is the fastest."

"And what are the two rules?" asked Bruce.

"Wear life jackets and don't go past the red buoys!" all the children shouted together.

The next three hours were great fun as all the children built their rafts, tried them out and then held races. One team never really got their raft to stay afloat for more than a few minutes at a time. Whatever they did, after a few paddles, the whole team would find themselves slipping into the water as their craft capsized once again. The other teams did better and the best one was Snowy Owl, the girls' team. This seemed to be down to Laura and Amelia who were very clever and sensible at designing and organising the team who worked very hard to make their raft a success. The twins in particular were fiercely determined to win the races and paddled furiously until they were red in the face. Tom and Ali agreed they had never seen them so serious and involved in anything before.

The Barn Owl team did quite well. Ali and Tom were made the leaders and they all worked well together, all except Jim who did everything they asked, but in slow motion. It took him so long to do anything that soon Ali and Tom stopped giving him instructions and he ended up sitting on the shore watching.

"Come on Jim," Mrs Barton said, "your team needs you."

Jim got up slowly and pretended to carry a plank of wood. But as soon as she had moved on he sat down again and watched, a smirk on his face as if he were thinking, "All this is for babies, I'm too grown up for this."

Once the raft was built, however, he was keen to get on it and paddle with the rest. The raft moved quite quickly through the water as the children paddled towards the blue buoys and soon they were ready to turn round and paddle back. Just as they reached the buoy bobbing in the water, Jim reached out and grabbed hold of it, pulling hard. The raft stopped suddenly with a jerk, and at the same time, Jim put out a foot and gave Sameer a nudge. Off balance, he rocked backwards and fell into the water with a scream. Although his life jacket kept his head above water, he looked terrified and flailed his arms around wildly. It was obvious he had no idea how to swim and just bobbed up and down helplessly in the water. Ali remembered the TV pictures he had seen on the news of refugees escaping from their countries in little boats and how sometimes, the boats were too full and capsized, tipping people out into the waves. For a moment Sameer looked just like one of those terrified people, and Ali wondered if this was how he and his family had come to England.

Quick as a flash, Tom, who was the nearest to Sameer, reached far down into the water and just about managed to reach Sameer's life jacket. Sameer was too frightened to try to get back onto the raft and so they paddled back slowly, dragging Sameer through the water behind them. Everyone on shore was laughing and cheering them on, not realising the seriousness of the situation.

"Well done," Bruce shouted, dragging Sameer out of the water and onto the shore. Having seen before what a great athlete Sameer was, he didn't notice that the boy was shaking and close to tears.

"Next time you'll have to hang onto the raft a bit tighter," he laughed. "Come on, here's a towel to dry off."

"But sir," stammered Tom, "he didn't just fall off, he was pushed."

"Yes," said Ali, "it wasn't an accident and it wasn't fun; it was deliberate."

"Now come on boys, don't be spoil-sports," smiled Bruce, "it's all just part of the challenge." He walked off giving Sameer's head a friendly pat.

"Yes, said Jim, walking past," it's all just part of the challenge."

Tom and Ali stood there speechless and then helping Sameer to get dry, Ali looked towards Tom in despair. What were they going to do? He had a terrible feeling that something dreadful was going to happen and that they were all powerless to prevent it.

Before each team left their raft moored at the edge of the lake, they were given a tin of paint and a brush and painted the name of their team on the side of it.

"Very important rule," announced Bruce seriously. "Absolutely no one is to even sit on any of these rafts, let alone paddle them on the lake unless we are here and have given you instructions to do so. Understood?"

"Yes," they all chorused. They stowed their life jackets in the shed at the water's edge and stood on the shore, shivering and dripping.

"Back to your dorms. Everyone is to have a hot shower and change into their pyjamas," announced Anne. "After the evening meal it's Pyjama Mini Olympics in the hall. Off you go everybody and be in the dining room by 6.15."

Jim had hurried off before the rest of the children. His head was in a spin. "Why did he keep on being so nasty to Sameer and why wasn't he good friends with the other boys anymore?" he wondered. He supposed it must be something to do with his Dad leaving home at the end of the holidays and going to live with another woman. He felt so angry and so sad and miserable all at the same time; he just wanted to lash out and hurt someone else and Sameer was an easy target. For some reason making someone else unhappy seemed to make him feel better. He decided he would try to be nicer to Sameer in the future.

But just then the boys arrived back to the dormitory and they were not in a good mood. Although they were cold and wet, that was not their first concern. It seemed that, without even speaking together, they had all decided that they were going to have to face Jim with his terrible behaviour and somehow get him to stop. They burst in through the door.

"What's wrong with you?" screamed Tom, going up to Jim and taking him by his wet T shirt and shaking him. "You could have really hurt Sameer. We're really fed up with you."

"Yes," agreed Ali, "we thought you were our friend but you're just being horrid and we're going to tell Mrs Barton all about you!" Arthur and Philip approached Jim too and poked him hard in the chest.

"We don't want you in our dormitory anymore," Arthur said.

Anger flared up in Jim in a huge surge and without thinking he lashed out at the boys, hitting Arthur in the mouth and knocking Ali to the floor.

"I don't care what you do," he shouted. "You're all little kids and I don't want anything to do with you anymore."

Then to everyone's surprise he burst into tears and rushed out through the door, muttering, "I'm sorry, I'm really sorry."

The boys were stunned. "We can't really tell on him now," said Tom, "he really seemed upset and sorry."

"Yes," agreed Arthur, rubbing his mouth," perhaps we'll give him one more chance."

By this time, the boys were shivering uncontrollably from their soaking in the lake and the most important thing seemed to be to have warm showers and get into dry clothes.

"Ok," let's see how we get on with him tonight," said Tom.

If they had known what would happen next, they might have done something different. But as it was, they decided to see if Jim really was sorry and would turn over a new leaf.

Chapter Eleven: A Disturbed Night

Pyjama Mini Olympics was great fun. There were sack races, egg and spoon races, hurdles, long jump, relay races and other team sports all done in their pyjamas and slippers. They kept on tripping over their pyjamas and losing their slippers so that even the fast runners ended up in tangled heaps on the floor laughing. The Barn Owl team seem to have recovered from their argument and got on well. Jim seemed to be trying hard to be nice to everyone and the boys breathed a sigh of relief; everything was going to be alright. The children were all tired after their energetic day and were quite glad when the leaders told them it was time for bed.

"Tomorrow we will spend the morning in the woods learning bush craft, and in the afternoon it's zorbing in the big field."

No one knew what zorbing was, "Just wait and see," said Anne laughing, "you'll love it."

Tucked up in their sleeping bags, the boys in Barn Owl Dormitory lay in the dark, waiting for sleep. All of a sudden there was a "Beep beep" and a light came on in Jim's bed.

"Hey, guys," whispered Jim, "do you fancy joining the girls in Snowy Owl Dorm for a midnight feast? Jill has just texted me to say they're ready for us!"

"What?" squeaked Tom, trying to keep his voice down. "What are you doing with a mobile phone? You know we're not allowed to have them here."

Indeed, that was one of the strictest rules, and one or two children who had brought their phones had handed them over Mrs Barton who would keep them until they were back at school.

"That's a silly rule," replied Jim quietly. No one will know, so it doesn't matter. See how useful they are. How else could Jill have told us the coast is clear?"

"Never mind the mobile phone rule," piped up Ali. "You know we're not allowed to go into each other's dorms at night either."

"Another silly rule," answered Jim, "So who's coming with me?" and he started to get out of his sleeping bag. "Or are you all scaredy cats?"

No one moved. "Oh, come on," mocked Jim, "you can't all be so pathetic. Come on Arthur, you come with me."

There was a long pause and then much to everyone's amazement Arthur struggled out of his sleeping bag, "Ok," he said, "I'll come."

The two boys crept over to the door together. "I've got my torch," said Jim, "just follow me."

The door creaked open and the boys were gone. "Night night scaredy cats," whispered Jim as he closed the door quietly.

Everyone lay in the dark, their ears straining to hear noises from Snowy Owl Dorm but there wasn't a sound. Minutes went by and the two boys didn't return. Slowly one by one, snug in their warm bags, and tired from the day's events the boys drifted off to sleep.

They were all in a deep sleep when shouts and screams from outside woke them up. Then the door crashed open and the light blazed on.

"Are the rest of you here?" shouted Mrs Barton. She was standing in the doorway, hair standing on end. "Is it only Jim and Arthur who are out of bed?"

Dazzled by the light and bleary from sleep the boys lay speechless as Mrs Barton looked at each bed.

"Well done boys, "she said, "I am pleased to see you have not been as stupid as Jim and Arthur. They will be spending the night in Bruce's room and I will be sleeping in Snowy Owl Dorm with the girls. We will sort this out in the morning. Go back to sleep. Good night."

With that, she flipped the light off, slammed their door, walked over to Snowy Owl Dorm and slammed that door too. All was quiet and dark again, but no one could get back to sleep.

"What do you think is going to happen to Jim and Arthur?" asked Tom.

"I don't know," said Sameer, "it seems such a shame about Arthur, he's usually so good."

"Yes, I think he just went to keep Jim company," answered Ali. "I wonder what will happen to the girls in Snowy Owl. I bet it was only Jackie and Jill that put them up to this. It really won't be fair if they all get into trouble."

They were soon to find out. At breakfast Mrs Barton stood up and announced, "I have very serious news for you all. Last night two boys from Barn Owl Dorm went into Snowy Owl Dorm for a midnight feast, invited in by two of the girls."

There was a gasp from the children as they looked round to see who the culprits were. Jim and Arthur were standing next to Mrs Barton, and on the other side were Jackie and Jill. They all looked miserable except Jim who was smiling.

"If that isn't bad enough, I was told by Jim that Jill had her mobile phone with her, which I have found and confiscated. Jill will not be allowed to join in any activities for the rest of the week and will spend her time working in the classroom. Unfortunately, the twins' parents are away visiting their grandmother, so I can't send them home. So Jackie, Jim and Arthur will miss this morning's activities but will join us after lunch. I am grateful to Jim for telling me about Jill's phone. I will be organising a search through everyone's belongings after lunch and there will be big trouble if I find any more phones."

The Barn Owl boys stared in horror at Mrs Barton and then at Jim who was still smiling. How dare he get Jill into trouble like that when his own phone was in their dormitory? And how was he going to hide it from the teachers when they searched through everyone's things?

"I am very disappointed in your behaviour," said Mrs Barton to the children standing next to her. "Think yourselves lucky that I have not been too hard on you." Then turning to the rest of the children she said, "And let this be a warning to you all. I will not be as kind next time."

The rest of breakfast was a very subdued affair and at the end of it, the twins, Jim and Arthur were led away to the classrooms by one of the assistants.

"Ok, kids, the rest of you have twenty minutes to get ready, tidy your dorms and be back here ready for a morning in the woods," announced Bruce. "You need to be wearing long-sleeved tops, jeans and sturdy footwear. Off you go."

They returned to Barn Owl Dorm and tidied up.

"I wonder where Jim's phone is," said Ali. "Do you think we should find it and hide it for him?"

"No, certainly not," the others said.

"It will serve him right when they find it," said Tom and then perhaps he'll be sent home early."

"That's a bit harsh, but it's certainly a relief that we don't have to worry about him being nasty to Sameer this morning," said Ali.

They all agreed with him, especially Sameer himseflf.

They all had a fantastic time in the woods. There was a competition to see who could build the best shelter from branches, twigs and other materials around them. When the shelters were finished, they sat in them to rest and eat their midmorning snack. Afterwards they learnt how to light a fire without matches by gathering dry twigs and grass, making a tinder nest and then shining a lens on it until a little spark was lit and they could nurture it into a flame.

"What a shame Arthur is missing this," said Sameer, "he would love it."

"Yes, I even feel a bit sorry for Jim, too, answered Ali," I just don't think he can help being horrid sometimes."

The boys would have been very surprised if they had known what Jim was up to at that time. He had asked the teaching assistant in the class room if he could go to the toilet. The toilet block was next to Barn Owl Dorm and he had quickly sneaked into the dorm and taken his phone from his sleeping bag where he had left it the night before. He knew he had to hide it before the dorm search and he had thought of just the place. Making sure he wasn't seen, he made his way down to the lake shore where the rafts they had made were still moored by the water's edge. It took him no time at all to pull in the Barn Owl raft, clamber aboard and hide the phone in between the barrels and under some rope. He knew no one would find it there and he could come back and get the phone after the dorm search. He then raced back to the class room where no one seemed to have noticed his absence.

The morning in the woods was finished by each team laying a trail for another team to follow. One team got totally lost and had to be rescued by Bruce, but on the whole the children thought they had successfully learnt to be Bush Crafters.

Chapter Twelve: Zorbing!

After lunch, all the children had to return to their dormitories while the teachers and leaders did a thorough search of them. The Barn Owl team stood in the middle of the hut whilst Mrs Barton searched through everyone's possessions. At any minute they expected her to find Jim's phone among his things but after a thorough search she said, "Well done children, no phones here, just a few chocolate bars which I am confiscating."

Ali felt very annoyed because he knew they were his Mars Bars which his Mum had packed in his bag, "… just in case you get peckish, dear," she had said.

They all tried not to look amazed that Jim's phone had not been found and waited for her to leave the hut with Ali's Mars Bars.

"Where's your phone?" they all asked Jim as soon as she had gone.

"Wouldn't you like to know?" Jim grinned. "You didn't think I'd let her find it did you? You all might be daft, but not me. Shame about your Mars Bars, Ali. Come on then, you need to find out what zorbing is all about."

With that he walked out of the hut but not without kicking one of Sameer's plastic bags hard as he went. Dirty clothes spilled out over the floor.

"Oh dear, we really will have to get you a proper bag, Sameer," he said, slamming the door behind him.

The boys stood stunned and then Ali started to help Sameer with his clothes.

"I can't believe it," said Arthur. "Wherever did he hide his phone, and just what is he going to do next?"

"I dread to think," answered Tom, "I don't have a good feeling about the rest of the day."

"Come on," said Sameer. "Don't let him spoil the day, and hurry up, we're going to be late!"

It turned out that zorbing was rolling round the field inside a huge transparent plastic ball! The children went in pairs and were fastened in tightly. Then they used their feet to roll the ball and steer it in the direction they wanted to go. The field sloped downwards and the ball rolled faster and faster unless they could control their speed with their feet.

Most of the children thought it looked great as Bruce and Anne demonstrated what you had to do to control the ball and roll around the field. But some of them looked worried and said they didn't like the idea of being trapped inside a huge ball which might roll where you didn't want to go. Surprisingly, Sameer was one of the ones who wasn't too keen on having a go.

"Now the children who feel a bit nervous will be paired up with someone more confident and you can go in a ball together," announced Anne. "Put up your hands if you would like to be paired with someone."

Jim's hand shot up and he called out, "I'd like to go with my friend Sameer. I've done this before so I should be able to help him."

The rest of the Barn Owl team looked horrified, and Sameer most of all. Jim had obviously seen that Sameer was nervous and was going to use the chance to make mischief.

"Thank you very much, Jim, that's very kind of you to help Sameer," called Anne. "You can go in this first ball here."

Sameer tried to protest but Anne ignored him and carried on organising the other children. Ali and his friends felt helpless to stop Jim and dreaded what might happen.

"Now these are the most important rules," announced Bruce. "Never go faster than your partner is happy with. If you want to go fast, you can see that the left side of the field is very steep. If you prefer a slower pace, stick to the right side of the field where there is a gentle slope. And always stay inside the marker cones down the sides of the field; we don't want any of you rolling away completely! Now fasten yourselves in and have a great time!"

Four pairs of children started to roll slowly down the slope in four huge transparent balls as the others looked on. They could see that the balls' speed and direction could be controlled by the people inside. The Barn Owl boys watched as Jim and Sameer's ball moved over to the steeper left side of the field and started to move quickly down the slope. Faster and faster it rolled and then suddenly veered off further to the left, ran over the cones and disappeared rapidly down a bank and over into the next field. Bruce and Anne set off running after it, followed by Mrs Barton and most of the children. The other three balls were still rolling slowly and carefully down the field and Tom and Ali dodged between them and raced over to where they could see Sameer and Jim lying in the bottom of their ball in a heap.

"Are you alright?" gasped Anne as she and Bruce opened the ball and peered inside.

Jim popped his head out grinning. "Oh sorry, he said, "we went a bit too fast. I'm fine but Sameer seems to be a bit upset for some reason."

Bruce leaned in and helped a trembling Sameer out of the ball. He was as white as a sheet and tears streamed down his face.

"I asked Jim not to go fast," he stammered, "but he just went faster and faster and was steering all over the place. He did it deliberately."

His legs seemed to collapse underneath him and he sat down suddenly and put his face in his hands. The boys gathered round him helplessly and then Ali turned on Jim.

"You knew that Sameer was nervous about going in the ball. Why did you go so fast and crash over the cones? You were deliberately trying to scare him."

"It's not my fault he's such a wimp," laughed Jim. He really needs to grow up a bit."

"Jim, that really is not very kind," said Bruce who was just beginning to realise that there was a problem between Jim and Sameer. "Apologise immediately."

"Sorry, Sameer," said Jim in a long drawn out drawl and with a shrug of his shoulders. He walked off with his hands in his pockets and made no attempt to help Sameer up or rescue the ball from the field.

"Right children," Bruce said nervously. "Help me get this ball back into position and then I think we'll just keep to the gentle side of the field. We don't want any more accidents."

Some of the children had been put off any zorbing and sat and watched as other, more adventurous ones had a go. But everyone was rather quiet and what should have been an enjoyable afternoon had been spoilt.

The boys sat with Sameer who soon cheered up and everyone was relieved to see he hadn't been hurt. They had been shocked by Jim's actions and were glad that the leaders had seen it too.

"I hope they can stop anything else happening between Jim and Sameer," said Tom. "It really is too nerve racking."

"Yes, I really feel that Jim will stop at nothing to be nasty to Sameer; he seems to be getting worse and worse," Ali replied.

As they sat there the sun stopped shining and the children saw that dark clouds were rolling in. A chilly breeze made them shiver and the boys felt even more nervous.

"Ok," said Bruce jumping up. It's time to go back. After dinner you're going to have the chance to practise your fire lighting skills and we will have a camp fire, toast marshmallows and sing some camp fire songs. Then we will do a short night walk in the woods before bed. That is if the rain holds off," he said doubtfully. "Let's hope it does. So off you go back to your huts and don't forget your torches and to get dressed warmly; it gets chilly at night, even around a camp fire."

As they neared their dormitory, the Brown Owl boys were surprised to see Jackie racing towards them, hair flying. She stopped in front of Jim and screamed at him.

"I hate you. You have spoilt it all for me and Jill. We always do everything together but you told on her about her mobile and now she's missing all the fun. Where did you hide your phone? I know you have one because Jill texted you. Just you wait. I'll get you for this!"

She stormed off leaving every one opened mouthed.

"Oh dear," said Jim, "she has got herself all hot and bothered."

"Well, it was really mean of you to tell Mrs Barton about Jill's phone," said Ali. "You knew it would get her into serious trouble."

"Yes, and where is your phone?" asked Tom. "Where have you hidden it?"

"Well that would be telling, wouldn't it?" answered Jim. "Come on everyone, you don't want to be late for dinner. And make sure Sameer is really wrapped up warm, we don't want him getting cold tonight, do we?"

Chapter Thirteen: The Vortex

The children gathered round in their teams to see who could start a fire first. This time they used batteries to make the first spark and then carefully coaxed the sparks into flames. It was one of the girls' teams who got their fire going first and so they were allowed to build it up with twigs and then branches until there was a fine blaze. The children sat around it toasting marshmallows and chatting happily together. It was fun to share this relaxing time together and Ali looked round at the faces of his friends, lit by the flickering fire light. His mother had been right, he was enjoying himself and he was so glad that he had come. He noticed that Jim and Sameer were sitting far apart, ignoring each other and he hoped they had seen an end to all the nastiness. Although Jackie was sitting with Laura and Amelia, she looked lonely without Jill and he wondered if she really would do something to get back at Jim.

The wind was getting up, blowing the flames this way and that and everyone hoped it wasn't going to rain. If it did they wouldn't be able to go on the Night Walk, which sounded rather exciting.

After half an hour of singing jolly songs Anne stood up and announced,

"Well everybody, torches at the ready! The rain is holding off so we can do the Night Walk in the woods. You must use your torches and keep to the main path. The idea is for you to experience how everything looks different at night and to see if you can use your newly learnt bush craft skills to find your way around. I will be in front of you all and Bruce will bring up the rear."

"Please try to stick with your dorm team, but don't worry if you get split up," added Bruce. "You must all be back in your dormitories by nine o'clock and we will come round half an hour later to check you are all in bed before lights out. Good luck!"

The children started off down the track into the woods, chattering excitedly. But as the lights from the centre faded, they realised how pitch black it was. There seemed to be no moon and dark clouds scudded along hiding any stars there may have been. They all switched on their torches and concentrated on following the feet in front of them and the path they were on. As they got deeper into the woods, the wind gusted strongly making the leaves rustle and rattle. Then there was the sound of rain on the leaves and it started pouring.

"Good," said Jim to himself, "perfect weather. No one will see me slip off down to the lake to get my phone from the raft. Mum will go mad if I lose it."

He quietly veered off the path towards the lake and soon found himself in deep undergrowth which was hard to push through. He thought that no one had seen him slip off, but he was wrong. Jackie had been following close behind him and when he turned off the path she followed him.

"What's he up to?" she thought. "No good I bet. I'm going to find out."

The two of them struggled through the rough grass and small bushes toward the lake. The sound of the wind in the trees, the rain beating down and his own shoes pushing through the undergrowth meant that Jim couldn't hear Jackie as she panted behind him.

It seemed to take ages, but eventually Jim felt the grass change to pebbles under his feet and he could hear the sound of water lapping the shore. He paused and shone his torch towards the rafts which were bobbing up and down wildly on the rough water.

"Now which is the Brown Owl raft?" he muttered to himself, "they all look the same." Suddenly he saw the writing on one of the rafts, "Brown Owl, that's it. Now all I have to do is crawl onto it and get the phone." He put his torch on the shore and started to clamber onto the raft. Jackie hung back so she wouldn't be seen.

"Whatever is he doing? He's being pretty silly getting on a raft without a life jacket on. Wherever is he going?" she wondered. Then it dawned on her. "He's not going anywhere; this is where he hid his phone, the sly fox. He's come back to get it. Well we'll see about that!"

She rushed forward, and just as Jim was lying on the raft feeling for his phone, she undid the rope and gave the raft a big shove with her foot. The raft shot forward away from shore and Jim screamed.

"Great, serves him right," thought Jackie. But then as she heard Jim yelling and saw the little raft rolling wildly from side to side on the rough water and drifting rapidly away from the shore, she realised what she had done.

"Hang on Jim", she yelled above the wind and rain. "Hang on. I'm going to get help."

Jim was terrified. Clinging onto a rocking, bobbing raft made of plastic barrels tied together with bits of rope, he was soon wet through and shivering. He could see nothing but black water swirling round him and realised he must be drifting towards the whirlpool and waterfalls they had been warned about. He reached down into the water and started to paddle for his life.

Jackie was in a panic. Following the beam of her torch, she ran back through the rough grass as fast as she could until she was back on the path in the wood. Her breath came in gasps, she had twisted her ankle and she was soaked through but all she could think of was how to get help. She realised that she and Jim would be in big trouble if the adults found out, so decided to ask the Brown Owl boys for help. She turned and ran towards the dormitories and arrived just as the last children were entering their huts.

"You have just over half an hour to get dry and ready for bed," she heard Bruce call out. "Anne and I will be round with hot drinks to warm you up before lights out."

"That gives us half an hour," thought Jackie.

She burst into the boys' hut and before they could say anything blurted out the whole story to them.

"You've got to come now," she said impatiently. "Come on, what are you waiting for?"

Without looking to see who was following her, Jackie raced off back towards the lake.

For a moment the boys stood staring at each other, speechless; then they all made a dash for the door.

"Hurry up!" called Jackie seeing them running behind her. "We've got to save him before the raft reaches the weir."

The boys had no idea what they were going to do.

"Don't you think we should tell the teachers?" panted Ali, "They'll know what to do."

"Don't be silly," argued Tom," that would get us all into trouble."

"We already are in trouble, "gasped Ali, "and how on earth are we going to rescue him?"

"Let's just get there and see what we can do," Sameer said as he overtook them and caught up with Jackie.

It was then they realised that Philip and Arthur weren't there.

"They must have stayed in the dorm, fancy not coming!" Ali said.

"They've obviously got more sense than we have," Tom said, "we must be mad."

With that the boys concentrated on running through the long grass without tripping up or losing their way. By the time they got to the lake they were gasping for breath, soaking wet and worn out. They stood on the shore but could see nothing on the dark waters. The wind was blowing hard and they could hear no sound from Jim.

Jackie was hopping up and down impatiently, "Hurry up," she yelled, "or it will be too late."

Ali looked hopelessly out into the dark, "It's no good," he said, "it's already too late. I'm not going out on a raft in this weather, it's far too dangerous. I'll go back and tell the leaders." With that he turned round and headed back up the shore, his head bent.

"I think he's right," sighed Tom, "if we did get on one of those rafts in this weather we would probably capsize. I'm not very good at paddling. It's just not safe. I think I'll go and help Ali raise the alarm." He too turned his back on the lake and set off back to the dorms.

Only Jackie was left to watch as Sameer appeared wearing a life jacket and carrying a wooden paddle.

"Quick," he said urgently, "once I'm safely on a raft, untie the rope and give me a gentle push out. Wait here for the leaders and keep on calling out so I'll know where to come back to."

Without hesitating he climbed onto the nearest raft, and as soon as it was free, began paddling out into the middle of the lake calling Jim's name as he went. Soon he had disappeared from sight and all Jackie could hear was Jim's name being called. And then there was nothing but the roar of the wind and the sound of rain falling and water rolling back and forth.

Jim was convinced he was going to die. He lay flat on the raft, helpless, his frozen fingers clutching the sides. He didn't dare move in case the raft capsized, and he had given up calling for help. He had watched helplessly as the raft had drifted past the blue buoys and now he knew he must be heading for the red buoys and beyond them, the whirlpool. It seemed he had been lying there for ever, when he heard a faint voice calling his name. At first he thought he was imagining it and then he heard it again, "Jim, where are you?"

"Here, over here," he croaked. He tried to sit up but the raft wobbled so dangerously, he lay down again quickly. Then he heard another sound. It was rushing water and at that moment the raft started to travel faster. He knew he was heading for the waterfalls and if the raft went over them he would be thrown off into the swirling, freezing water.

Then he heard the voice again, "Jim, I can see you. Lean over and hang onto the weeds at the side of the lake. Hang on and you won't go over the waterfall."

Jim lifted his head and sure enough, his raft was rushing past a big clump of weeds. He tried to grab them as he raced past, faster and faster. He missed the first time but on the second attempt managed to grab a handful of grass. The raft slowed down suddenly and then swung round so that his feet were facing the weir. But then the raft started to spin madly round and round and he realised he was caught in the whirlpool. The vortex of water seemed to be pulling him down as well as around. His hands were so cold he couldn't feel the weeds but he hung on for dear life, his arms being pulled as the water spun around and tried to carry him over the weir. Just then he saw a figure on a raft, paddling furiously towards him.

"Hang on, I'm nearly there, don't let go," yelled the voice.

But Jim was so cold and tired, and the water was pulling him round so hard that he started to lose his grip on the weeds. Just as he let go and his raft sped towards the waterfall, a  strong arm grabbed him and hauled him towards the other raft. For a moment the two rafts hung together in the water and then Jim's raft slipped away and he managed to cling on to the other one and pull himself onto it.

"Hang on," gasped his rescuer, "I've got to paddle." His arms flashed and the paddle churned the water but at first it seemed this raft too would slide over the waterfall. But gradually they broke away from the pull of the water and started to move away from danger. Jim lay with his eyes shut, hardly daring to believe he might be safe, as his rescuer continued to move them to safety. When they got to the first set of buoys the paddler wrapped his feet round a buoy, steadied the raft and took off his life jacket.

"Here," he panted, "put this on, the water will be quite rough when we get to the shore and you might fall in."

It was then that Jim realised who his rescuer was.

"Sameer," he gasped, "you've saved me. You don't even like water and you can't swim, but you have saved me, after all I have done to you."

"Never mind about that," said Sameer. "You needed help so I helped you, what else could I have done? Come on, let's get back to the others."

Jim lay back on the raft and watched as his true friend and rescuer paddled him back to safety. He could hardly take in what Sameer had done for him, of all people. It really was amazing. He knew he didn't deserve it and would never be able to repay him. But then he knew that Sameer didn't want repaying. Sameer had saved him because that was the sort of person Sameer was.

Everyone was on the beach to meet them. The children all cheered as Sameer helped his friend off the raft and then helped him to take off his life jacket. Then the adults rushed forward with blankets and hugs and hot drinks. They were just so relieved that all the children were safe that they gave no thought to telling anyone off that night. Everyone trooped back to the dormitories and soon all the children were tucked up in bed.

Chapter Fourteen: The Good Friend

The boys in Barn Owl Dorm were incredibly relieved to be back, safe and warm in their sleeping bags. The incidents of the night had shaken them. The fear and the darkness had almost overwhelmed them.

"I'm sorry I didn't try to help you, Jim," whispered Ali.

"We are too," Arthur, Tom and Philip said together.

"I'm the one who's sorry for spoiling everyone's time here," mumbled Jim, "and especially for being so horrible to you Sameer; thank you for rescuing me."

No one said anything else. There was nothing else to say. The boys of Barn Owl Dorm knew they were a team at last.

The next day Jim and the twins apologised to each other and Mrs Barton gave them all a good talking to. Then the manager of the centre summoned Jim and Sameer to his office for a severe telling off.

"You, Jim broke all our rules by getting on a raft without a life jacket and with no adult supervision," he growled sternly. "And Sameer, you took far too big a risk by paddling out to rescue him by yourself. You are both banned from participating in any water sports at Princefield ever again. Let that be a lesson to you to never take a risk where water is concerned. Now off you go and enjoy the rest of your final day here."

Their last day was fun indeed. While some of the children went kayaking and canoeing on the lake, the others kept Sameer and Jim company as they clambered through the tree tops on an aerial walk way in the woods. Jim was especially glad to spend time with his friend Sameer, Jackie was reunited with Jill and the others were just pleased they were all together again. It seemed that at last the Fern Valley Venturers had become the great team they were meant to be.

At the end of the day, as the bus drew out of Princefield, Sameer asked cheerfully,

"When can we come again?"

"Very soon, I hope!" laughed Mrs Barton and all of Class Four agreed.

Can you tell that The Vortex is a modern retelling of The Parable of the Good Samaritan?

Check out Luke 10 verses 30-37 in the Bible to see what you think.

The hidden meaning of the parable is that Jesus loved the people who hated him as much as he loved his friends, and wants us to do the same.

* Do you think God is friends with you, and you with him?

The Villa

Chapter One: The Digger

There was great excitement in Fern Valley Village. A huge yellow digger was due to come trundling onto Farmer Cooper's land where it would start to scrape off the surface of one of the large wheat fields on the farm.

"Come on, hurry up," called Jackie to Jill, "you're going to miss it!"

"I'm coming as fast as I can," yelled her sister, "Jim and Sameer are on their way too."

The four children arrived just in time to watch as the mighty machine rolled down the main street of the village on its large caterpillar treads. It was a tight squeeze down the lane to the farm entrance and the children watched with bated breath as it inched slowly forward through the gate of Cooper's Farm, its big excavating bucket swinging, and the caterpillars churning up the ground. It juddered over the cobblestones of the farmyard and only came to a halt when it reached the field where it was due to start work. Others had followed the digger onto the farm and were gathering round it excitedly. Suddenly Farmer Cooper appeared and started waving his arms furiously.

"Hey, everyone, off my land, you're trespassing," he shouted. He was a short, fat man with a dark red face, weathered from a life time working outdoors, and his thick beetle brows were set in an ugly frown.

"Who said you could come stomping onto my land?" he continued. "I've no choice but to let the archaeologists onto my farm, but the rest of you can make yourselves scarce. I'm not having the whole village coming to gawp. Now go away."

Everyone moved slowly back into the lane, leaving only the driver of the digger to clamber down from the cab.

"Right you are Mr Cooper, the team will be here to start first thing tomorrow morning," he said cheerily, ignoring Farmer Cooper's scowling face. "See you bright and early."

"Poor Farmer Cooper," said Jim, "he really doesn't want an archaeological dig messing up his fields."

"I know, but he has no choice," replied Jackie, "and it's lucky for us; it should make the holidays really interesting."

"As long as Farmer Cooper lets us come and watch what's going on," Sameer said doubtfully. "We'll just have to wait and see."

Chapter Two: A Few Bits of Pottery in a Wheat Field

It had all started a few weeks ago. The Coopers' farm buildings lay nestled in a fold in Fern Valley, sheltered from the worst of the winds and rains. Their wheat fields were on higher ground and sloped down to the river which snaked its way through the valley. For several years, young Jed Cooper who farmed the land with his father had noticed that the wheat in one of the fields always grew in a strange way. There seemed to be lines of wheat which didn't grow as tall as the rest of the crop, making a sort of pattern in the field. Doing some research he found that some people thought these crop markings were made by aliens! But most thought it meant there were some old walls buried underneath the soil. He had mentioned it to his father who had told him to stop day-dreaming and get on with the work. This year the wheat had already been harvested from this field leaving stubble and rough soil and Jed and his father had been walking carefully round the field looking for the best spot to build some holiday cottages. The farm didn't make a lot of money and Farmer Cooper hoped to earn extra cash from people who wanted to spend a few days holiday in the peace and beauty of the countryside. Jed thought this was an awful idea but his father took no notice of him and was determined to have the cottages built as soon as possible. As they were walking around, Jed scuffed at the ground and his foot came up against something hard. Bending down and scraping away at the soil he saw a small, dark red stone sticking out of the ground. He scraped away excitedly and then

124

carefully pulled it out. It wasn't a stone; even he could tell it was a bit of pottery with some kind of pattern on it.

Jumping up excitedly he called his dad over, "Look, Dad, look, it's some sort of pottery, maybe from a jug or a bowl. Perhaps there really are old buildings under here and perhaps this is part of someone's cup from long ago!"

"Don't be daft, lad, it's probably just a broken mug from when one of us was working in the field," growled Farmer Cooper. "And don't you be telling anyone about it. I've heard what happens when people find old stuff on their land. Those stupid archaeologists have to come and investigate. They dig everything up and make a mess and a huge fuss and even worse, it means you can't get on with what you want to do. We need to build those cottages, so throw that away and keep quiet. Don't you dare say a word to anyone, I'm warning you!"

"But Dad," started Jed, but then he saw his father's furious face and stopped. Without his father noticing, he put the piece of pottery safely in his jacket pocket and the two farmers returned to the farmhouse.

Jed looked nothing like his father. He was taller and thinner, his hair was fairer and his face was more friendly and cheerful. But he had the same stubborn streak as his father and once he made his mind up to do something nothing would stop him. And he had decided to find out about his piece of pottery. So the next day, Jed took his find to the Archaeology Department of the University in town and found that he had indeed discovered some rather fine Roman pottery. Within days a team of archaeologists was tramping round Cooper's Farm. They found more pieces of pottery and even some large grey stones which were probably from an ancient building and, just as Farmer Cooper had feared, they decided that his field would be the site of The University Summer Dig.

"You're not coming here, digging up my field just to find some stupid old buildings," Farmer Cooper had yelled at the surprised archaeologists. "It's new ones I'm interested in building and I don't want you lot getting in my way and slowing me down."

But it seemed that he had no choice and would have to wait until the excavation was finished before he could start building his cottages.

"Don't worry Sir, we'll only be here for a week or two to start with over the summer," the head archaeologist had said. "But of course if we find a Roman building you might not be able to build your cottages there......." He had stopped speaking when he saw Farmer Cooper's furious face and had hurried away.

There were rumours that Farmer Cooper was so angry with his son that he had thrown Jed out of the house and told him never to come back. It was true that Jed hadn't been seen in the village for days and a new man had been hired to work on the farm.

The news of the find had spread like wild fire round the village and so it was that the twins Jackie and Jill and their friends Sameer and Jim had been out to meet the digger which would scrape off the top layer of the field ready for the archaeologists to start digging.

"I can't believe it," said Jim, "a real archaeological dig in our village!"

"Yes, and a Roman one too," added Jill, "that's nearly two thousand years ago. I wonder what they'll find."

"Well," said Jackie, "I'm going to ask if we can help. It's the holidays after all; we've nothing else to do. What do you say; do you want to join in?"

"You bet!" the three children chorused excitedly.

"What a shame Ali and Tom are away on holiday," said Sameer, "they'll miss all the fun."

"Yes, it's a shame all The Fern Valley Venturers won't be here to enjoy this adventure," said Jill, but let's ask Laura and Amelia to join in too." The others agreed.

"Right, be here first thing tomorrow morning," said Jackie. "They start early and we want to be in on it from the beginning, don't we?"

Chapter Three: The Labourers are Hired

The six children were at the farm bright and early. They were all in the same class at Fern Valley Junior School and had become firm friends since an eventful four days at their school activity camp earlier in the year. As usual the twins were dressed identically and jumping around excitedly. The other two girls were quieter and more serious and were the best of friends; where one went, the other went too. The same could be said of Jim and Sameer; at one time fierce enemies, they were now inseparable.

"Just look at all those people," exclaimed Jill as they arrived at the field. "What are they all doing here?"

"Some of them will be the main archaeologists from the university and some will be their students who have come along to learn and help with the dig," Laura replied knowledgeably.

"Oh, I hope they'll want us," said Amelia doubtfully.

Just then a large man approached them smiling broadly. His long grey hair was flying everywhere and on top of it was perched an old, brown, scruffy hat. His jeans were already muddy and his brightly coloured T-shirt had seen better days. They found out later that this was the head of the archaeology department who would be leading the dig. His name was Oliver.

"And what can I do for you?" he called cheerfully. "Have you just come to gawp or are you going to get in the way as well?"

"Oh please," said Jim in his politest voice, "we were wondering if you would let us work on the dig with you. We'd work very hard and do what you told us to do."

"Yes," said Laura, "we've got very interested in the Romans since we did them at school and we'd love to find out more."

"It'd be so cool," chipped in Jackie, "we might even find some dead bodies or a pile of treasure!"

The others were annoyed with Jackie but Oliver threw back his head and roared with laughter.

"Ok, you six. We could do with some help. But this is going to be no picnic. We will expect you here every morning at half past seven and we don't finish until five o'clock. There will be no sitting around, it is hard physical work and you will have to follow all instructions carefully. We will give you a lot of responsibility and you will have to be very sensible and careful. You never know what finds we might make and we don't want anyone messing things up. Understood?"

The children looked a bit startled; perhaps this was going to be harder than they had expected. Seeing their doubtful faces, Oliver burst out laughing.

"Don't look so worried, it's not that bad. And if you work well there is a reward! At the end of the dig we will be re-enacting a day in the life of a Roman family and making a film of it. You will be able to dress up in Roman costumes and take part in the film. Well, what do you think of that?"

"Oh wow!" screamed Jill and Jackie together. "That's fantastic!"

The others all agreed, any doubts disappearing as they thought of being in a film.

"Well off you go!" said Oliver. "I want written permission from your parents and you'll need to wear boots, jeans, long sleeved tops and hats. Bring sun cream, bottles of water and a packed lunch. Hurry up or you'll miss the geo-phys man doing his survey before the digger takes off the top layer of earth. I'll give you half an hour!"

"Who on earth is Joe Fizz?" asked Jim as the children hurried home.

"Don't you know anything?" Laura giggled. "He didn't say Joe Fizz; he said geo phys. It means a geo-physical survey. It's a sort of machine which sends radar into the ground and it makes a sort of picture so they can see where there are underground walls and things so they can decide where to dig," she replied rather grandly.

"You sound as if you have swallowed an encyclopaedia," Jim said, "I don't know how you know all this stuff."

"Stop talking and hurry up," said Jill, "or we'll miss Joe Fizz and the digger."

The children were soon back at the field and watched as a man walked up and down pushing a machine in front of him.

"It looks like one of those machines the school caretaker uses to paint the white lines on the football pitch," said Sameer, "I can't see what good that will do."

Back and forwards went the man until he had walked over the whole field. The archaeologists then huddled together over pieces of paper and waved their arms around excitedly.

"I don't know why they're getting so excited, this is really boring," complained Jackie. But just then the digger roared into life and started to scrape off the stubble and top soil of a corner of the field. The bucket clanked down, dragged along and then lifted its load, dumping it in a pile to one side.

"The geo-phys must have found something there," said Sameer. He was fascinated by the skill of the operator as he pulled various levers and made the huge machine do just what he wanted. In no time at all, the digger had cleared a square of bare soil several metres wide and was trundling back over to the farm yard, its job done.

Oliver came hurrying over to the children. "Well, it's very good news. The survey showed up what we think must be buried walls. The digger has cleared the ground and now we are going to dig some trenches to see if we can find them. It's time to get to work. It's two of you kids to each adult. Do exactly what they tell you to do and no slacking, you're here to work." He hurried off, waving a trowel around in the air.

Looking round, the children realised they weren't the only ones there from the local schools. Several teenagers were already hard at work shovelling soil into a pile.

"Isn't that boy from your brother's class?" Jim asked Laura, recognising a tall thin boy with masses of black hair down to his shoulders. "Isn't he the one who's always in trouble?"

"Oh yes," replied Laura, surprised. "It's Colin. I don't know what he's doing here. I shouldn't think he's interested in archaeology."

"Probably up to no good, if you ask me," said Jill. "I've heard his dad is always in trouble with the police."

"Just because his dad's not very nice doesn't mean he's the same," said Amelia.

"I wouldn't be so sure about that," said Jim, "I think we'd better keep an eye on him."

Their conversation was interrupted by one of the archaeologists.

"Test pits first," he said. "We will dig holes in several places to see if we can find any evidence of a building being here. Each group will make a one metre square hole. All the soil goes on the spoil heap which we will look through later. So get those gloves and trowels and start to scrape."

The children were amazed to find that they had to kneel down and gently scrape away at the soil with a small garden trowel making a pile of soil to one side, and all the time looking for anything that their trowels might reveal.

"This is going to take absolutely ages," said Jill.

"Yes and I heard one of them say we have to dig down at least a metre," replied Jackie, it's going to take all day!"

"Better get to work then," said Laura. "I hope I find some pottery or something."

"Huh, I'm only interested in finding treasure," Jim replied. "Some gold coins or something."

"You'll be lucky," one of the archaeologists chuckled. "Come on, get working!"

The next three hours crawled by as, on their hands and knees, they all scraped and scraped and scraped. Their knees soon went numb and their hands ached with the effort of gripping their trowels. When they got up to carry the soil to the pile nearby they were so stiff they could hardly stand up straight and their backs ached as they dragged the buckets of soil along and emptied them onto the mound. To make matters worse, the day got hotter and hotter and sweat was soon streaming down their faces, mixing with the smudges of dirt they were covered in. No one found anything of interest and by lunch time the children were completely fed up.

"I don't know how much more I can take of this," moaned Jim as he sprawled out under a tree, taking great swigs from his water bottle.

"This isn't what I signed up for," Jackie groaned. "If we don't find anything this afternoon I'm giving up."

"What a boring job," agreed Sameer. "These archaeologists must be mad."

"I think we ought to thank them and tell them we aren't coming back tomorrow," suggested Amelia. Everyone but Laura agreed.

"You never know," she said enthusiastically, "we might be digging up a beautiful Roman building. Remember, they have those beautiful mosaics on the floor. We might find one of those!"

"You must be joking!" answered Jim, "I think I might go home now, I've had enough."

Just then Oliver approached the hot and miserable group.

"Don't look so fed up," he laughed, "we've only just started. You have to be patient. Come on, don't give up. This afternoon you've got a different job. I want you to sieve the soil from the spoil heap in those big sieves and see if there is anything we have missed. Come on, chop chop, there's work to be done!"

Chapter Four: Tesserae!

The children didn't know which was worse, the morning's scraping or the afternoon's sieving. Their arms were soon aching from lifting the heavy buckets of soil and then shaking the soil through the garden sieves. Once again, they found absolutely nothing and were just about to give up when there was a shout from the bottom of one of the pits.

"Stones, coloured stones!"

The children raced to the pit and peered in. An archaeologist was crouching in one corner, waving his trowel excitedly.

"I can't see what he's getting so excited about," said Sameer, "what's good about a few muddy stones?"

"They might be tesserae," Laura said seriously.

"Tessa who?" asked Jim doubtfully, "who are you talking about?"

"Where were you when we learnt about the Romans?" asked Laura. "You say it like tessa- ray. They're the little stones which make up the mosaic floors of Roman villas. We must have found a villa!"

"Gosh!" the others exclaimed.

Just then Oliver arrived, "Stand back from the edge; let's see what we have here!" He jumped down into the pit, clutching a bottle of water and a scrubbing brush. He poured water onto the stones and carefully brushed the mud away. To their astonishment, the small brown squares of stone turned blue and white and they could see that they made a pattern. The archaeologists carried on scraping, brushing and cleaning until the children could see that it really was a beautifully decorated floor of blue and white stones forming a geometric pattern. The archaeologists worked out which way the floor would continue and decided to make a large trench the next day.

"We should be able to follow the rest of the floor and find some walls tomorrow," Oliver explained. "We'll photograph and document this and then cover it up to protect it. But come on, we've another couple of hours of work before we pack up."

The children groaned and returned to their sieving. The sun was still beating down strongly even at the end of the day and seemed to drain all their strength and energy away. The wonderful find had encouraged them but they still couldn't wait to go home. The older boys seemed to have given up and were lounging around on the grass, drinking from their water bottles and Jackie noticed that Colin seemed to have disappeared altogether.

"What a lazy lot," she thought, "and I wonder where that Colin's got to."

There was still an hour to go when Jim who was sieving with Sameer spotted something in the soil.

"What's that?" he cried. There in the sieve lay two small, round dirty objects. Before they could call Oliver over, one of the students shouted, "Coins, we've found some coins!"

As people rushed towards their trench, the two boys found several more coins and then a whole pile of them. Oliver rushed over with his bottle of water and little brush and was soon expertly cleaning each object to reveal they were indeed coins with a man's head engraved on one side.

"That looks like Emperor Julian," he gasped. He could hardly contain his excitement. "This is an amazing find, well done boys, well done. As you found them I want you to carry on cleaning them up and then put them in this finds tray. One of the students can document them for us. This really has been a fantastic start to our dig; all this on only our first day!" He walked off shaking his head in disbelief.

It took Jim and Sameer the rest of the afternoon to clean the coins and put them in the tray. Altogether there were thirty coins of different sizes but all with the same head engraved on them. Their boredom and tiredness had completely disappeared. They laid the last of the coins in the tray and went over to join the others who were lying on the ground, filthy and exhausted.

"I can't believe you really did find treasure," laughed Amelia. "You're so lucky."

"Yes, it's really not fair," Laura said quietly. "You know absolutely nothing about the Romans and you're the one to make such a great find. It should have been me." She looked close to tears.

"Oh come on," laughed Jim; "don't be such a spoil sport. I found something today; you'll probably find a gold crown tomorrow and then you can boast all you like!"

"Come on you two, stop bickering," Amelia said. "All I'm interested in is going home, I'm starving. Come on, get your things."

"Yes, hurry up, all the other helpers have already gone," said Jill.

"No they haven't," Laura answered, "look, that boy Colin is still here; what is he doing?"

The children looked up to see Colin walking quickly away from the hut where the tools and finds were being kept. His hands were thrust deep into his pockets and his long hair hid his face from view.

"That's strange," said Jackie; "I'm absolutely sure he went home ages ago. He wasn't with his friends. I wonder why he's come back?"

"You're imagining things," Jim said, "why would he go home and come back again?"

As they watched Colin hurry out of the field, they saw a rough looking man appear from behind the hedge and meet him. The two bent their heads together and then the man slapped Colin on the back and smiled.

"That's Colin's dad," said Laura, "I wonder what he's doing here."

"Never mind them," said Sameer impatiently, "come on; let's go home before we starve to death."

"Or die of exhaustion," agreed Amelia.

They waved goodbye to Oliver who was tidying up and locking the hut.

"Well done, kids, see you tomorrow bright and early!"

"I'm not so sure about that," groaned Jill, "it's too much like hard work, I might give it a miss." There were a few murmurs of agreement but in the end it was decided that those who wanted to carry on would meet by the farm gate at twenty past seven the next morning. As they said their goodbyes, each of them wondered who would actually turn up the following day.

Chapter Five: Vandalism and Theft!

The day was already warm when five out of six children met at the farm gate the next morning. This time they were better prepared. They each had big bags stuffed full of food and drink, blankets to sit on, mats to kneel on and sunglasses to keep the glare out of their eyes.

"So it's only Jill who's given up," said Amelia.

"Yes," Jackie replied, "I left her snoring in bed; she's such a lazybones!"

As soon as they walked onto the field they knew something was wrong. No one was working and Oliver and the rest of the archaeologists were gathered round the trench where the mosaic floor had been found, peering into it. They all had serious expressions on their faces.

"Who's done this?" roared Oliver. His normally cheerful face was twisted in anger. "This is vandalism!"

The children rushed over and to their horror saw that the trench had been completely filled in with soil and a layer of stones and rubbish had been heaped on top. Wheelbarrows, trowels and other equipment had been thrown around all over the site and a large sign painted in red letters stood in the middle of the chaos. "KEEP OFF" it said.

"Get all this cleared up," yelled Oliver, "I want this trench dug out again and everything back to where it was yesterday. I'm going to pay a visit to Farmer Cooper." With that he stormed off and everybody leapt into action.

"Do you think Farmer Cooper would do this?" asked Sameer.

"Well he certainly didn't want the dig on his land, but I don't think he would go as far as this," replied Jim.

"Come on kids; lend us a hand," growled one of the archaeologists; "you're not here to natter."

And so they all got to work. It took half the morning to tidy up and dig out the trench again and by the end of it everybody was exhausted. Oliver had returned with Farmer Cooper who seemed as mystified as everyone else.

"Well, I just want you lot off my land as fast as possible, so why would I do this? It'll mean you'll be here even longer now," he grunted crossly. "I'll leave a couple of the dogs out here tonight to guard the place. That should stop any more monkey business. Now I've got work to do." He stomped off angrily muttering under his breath.

"Perhaps it's something to do with Colin and his dad," Jackie suggested. "Look, he doesn't seem at all worried about what's happened." Indeed, Colin was lounging around with his friends, laughing and joking and waving a huge sandwich around in between taking bites of it and gulps from a Coke bottle. The sight of them seemed to annoy Oliver. "Hey you lot. You can either get to work or go home; we don't need you cluttering up the place."

Colin grinned but got slowly to his feet, "Come on lads, the slave driver's cracking his whip!" He spoke quietly enough for Oliver not to hear him. Colin's friends laughed but the younger children were shocked.

"I don't know what he's doing here," Laura said. "He doesn't seem at all interested in the dig."

"And I can't see him wanting to get dressed up in Roman costume either," said Jim. He's up to no good, mark my words."

The rest of the morning was spent with more trowelling and sieving for the children. A new trench was opened up and walls were found but no new finds. It was even hotter than the day before and once more the children were beginning to wonder why they were there when there was a shout from the bottom of the new trench.

"Pottery, I've found a pot and it's not broken," called one of the students. Running over, the children could see a large pot with a pattern round the rim, still half buried in the soil. As they watched, the student scraped away carefully until he gently lifted up a round bottomed pot and held it up for everyone to see.

"That's a beauty!" said Oliver. "One of you kids, go to the shed and get a finds tray to put it in; this is a great find, a storage pot that hasn't been broken. Amazing!"

Jim hurried over to the shed. He had to admit he was enjoying this archaeology thing more than he had expected. As he entered the gloom of the shed to get a finds tray, he noticed the tray with the coins he had found yesterday sitting safely on a shelf. Feeling pleased with himself he peered into the tray to admire his find but nearly dropped the tray in astonishment. Some of the coins had gone! Letting his eyes get used to the gloom he carefully counted the coins. There were only twenty and yesterday there had been thirty. Not believing his eyes, he counted them again, and then again but sure enough, ten were missing. He bent down and searched on the ground and under the shelves but found nothing.

"Oliver or one of the other archaeologists has probably taken them to study them better," he thought. "I won't say anything because it'll look as if I don't trust them."

Making sure the coins were safely back on the shelf he quickly grabbed a finds tray and hurried out of the shed.

"Hurry up lad, what've you been doing in there?" Oliver laughed. "We haven't got all day; hand the tray over." He carefully laid the pot in the tray and instructed one of the students to clean and label it.

It was lunch time at last and the children spread out their blankets and flung themselves down wearily. As they ate their delicious picnics they discussed the vandalism and came to the conclusion it had been one of the gangs from town who had nothing better to do than spoil things for other people. Jim didn't mention the missing coins. Although it was still baking hot and the sun was still beating down, he felt a shiver go up and down his spine. Something was wrong and he felt as if the day had gone bad.

After eating a huge sandwich, a bag of crisps, two apples and a banana, Jackie jumped up.

"I'm just going for a stroll," she said, and quickly disappeared behind the hedge. Less than two minutes later she reappeared.

"Hey, Colin's dad is just down the lane, "she said. "He's not doing anything, just sitting there under a bush and he looked annoyed when we saw him. I wonder what he's doing."

"No idea," yawned Amelia, "I suppose if he's no job to go to he's just hanging around bored."

"Looked jolly suspicious to me," replied Jackie, tucking into another huge sandwich and bag of crisps.

Suddenly Laura laughed, "You're the suspicious one. How can you eat another sandwich after all you've just had, and why did you say he looked annoyed when *we* saw him? You're not Jackie, you're Jill!"

"I wondered how long it would take you to realise," laughed Jill at the bewildered children. "Jackie and I decided we would take it in turns to work on the dig. It's Jackie in the morning and me in the afternoon. That way we'll both have a go but not get too tired, it's just too much like hard work! And it worked, only Laura noticed; it's such good fun tricking you all!"

They all screeched and leapt on her, amused and annoyed at the same time that the twins had fooled them once again.

"Shhh," hissed a voice behind the hedge, "you're making too much noise and Oliver will hear you and wonder what's going on."

Jackie's furious face peered through the leaves at them which only made the children laugh even louder.

"Well make yourself useful then and keep an eye on Colin's dad," Laura said, "we're sure he's up to no good."

Jackie disappeared and the children lay down to rest. Even under the trees it was sweltering and everything seemed to shimmer and dance above the field. The air felt still and heavy and sounds seemed dull and muffled. There was a smell of warm earth and sweet grass.

"This is just too hot," moaned Jill. "I'm worn out and I haven't even done anything yet!"

"How do you think we feel then?" groaned Amelia. "Come on everybody, it's time to get back to work."

Chapter Six: More Finds

The next two hours were spent in more back-breaking work in the trenches. One of the students was excavating the mosaic floor and the girls helped with their trowels, scraping and scraping at the soil and revealing more of the beautiful patterned floor.

"This must have been a really posh house to have such a lovely big floor," remarked Laura.

"Pity the poor slaves who had to clean it every day," said Jill. "We're a bit like modern day slaves, working away for no money. It's so hot down here I think I'm going to melt."

"Well at least we're going to get dressed up and be in a film," Amelia laughed; "they wouldn't have been able to do that."

"Huh, I bet I'll have to play one of the slaves," said Jill. "You'll probably be the lady of the house swanning around in a lovely toga and I'll be washing your feet!"

Just then Laura's trowel hit something. She carefully scraped away the soil around it and to her astonishment saw a small, delicate object lying on the mosaic floor. Picking it up carefully she saw it looked like a piece of jewellery. Although it was still covered in dirt she could see three thin delicate strands of metal attached to a pin at the back.

"A brooch, I've found a brooch!" she screamed in delight. The student came over with a bottle of water and a little brush and carefully cleaned it until they could all see it was indeed a beautiful metal brooch.

"Well this is just the sort of thing your lady of the house would have been wearing as she swanned around the place in her posh toga," she laughed. "She would have used it to fasten her cloak. Let's call Oliver over."

The brooch was labelled and put in a finds tray and within an hour four more brooches and several hair pins had joined it. The girls were so excited that all their aches and pains disappeared as they eagerly looked for more evidence of a wealthy Roman lady's jewellery collection. Between them they found some buckles from a belt, two bracelets and another brooch.

"It's like she had a jewellery box with all this stuff in. I wonder why she didn't take it with her when she left," the student mused.

Meanwhile, the boys had been helping to dig out the walls of the building which Oliver declared was definitely a Romano- British villa where a wealthy British farmer had lived with his family and slaves. He had started to live like the Romans did and lived in a Roman style house with poor British slaves doing all the hard work.

"Not much fun for them," grunted Jim as he rubbed his aching hands together. "I'm beginning to understand what they must have felt like!"

"Ok, time for a break," called Oliver;" you've got twenty minutes."

The children collapsed in a heap under the trees, the girls talking excitedly about their finds, and the boys complaining that they'd found nothing.

"Psst!" Jackie's head appeared through the leaves of the hedge behind them. "Colin's dad is still hanging around in the lane, and now Colin has joined him. They're whispering together and now they're both going off together."

"Seems pretty fishy to me," said Jim, "and you did say yesterday that he disappeared in the afternoon and then came back as we were all leaving."

"I knew I was right," Jackie replied. "I'll stay here and if I see them coming back I'll do one of my barn owl calls and I'll watch his dad and you can see what Colin gets up to."

"Great idea," whispered Jim, "now go away before someone wonders why I am talking to a hedge!"

"You two think you're Sherlock Holmes and Dr Watson," said Laura scornfully. "You're making a mystery out of nothing. As if being on this dig isn't exciting enough."

"Well, I think there's something in it," said Sameer. "We still don't know who made all that mess this morning; it could be Colin and his dad."

"Why on earth would they want to do that?" asked Amelia. "It seems so pointless."

"That's what vandalism is," replied Sameer, "pointless."

"More to the point," thought Jim, "is that no one knows who stole the coins because no one even knows yet that they've been stolen."

His troubled thoughts were interrupted by Oliver's call to work.

"We've a couple more hours to go before we pack up," he said cheerfully. "Who knows what we'll find next; this is all going so well. Back to where you were working before, and you girls see if you can find something more from our Roman lady's lost jewellery box," he chuckled.

Jim and Sameer returned to the walls which now seemed to be bending round into an L shape. Jim noticed that Colin had indeed disappeared and he kept a sharp ear open for Jackie's barn owl call.

As they worked the sun beat down on their backs as if it wanted to press them down into the ground. There wasn't even a breath of wind and the air seemed hazy with heat. All that could be heard was the scraping of trowels and the grunts of hot and weary people and then a triumphant cry from Amelia,

"I've found something too!" It was in fact a necklace with fancy engraving on it and a little later the student dug up some more brooches and pins.

"Well our Roman lady was certainly fond of her jewellery!" exclaimed Oliver, "I've not seen such a collection before." He was looking at the clean, shiny objects lying in the finds tray, each one labelled and catalogued in the finds book.

Even the boys had found pieces of pottery at the bottom of one of the walls, which Oliver had said were fine specimens of fourth century Romano-British pottery.

"Gosh!" exclaimed Sameer, "that means they're nearly two thousand years old."

"I wonder if anyone will find my Superman mug two thousand years from now," Jim thought. He was beginning to think that he'd done enough hard work for one day when he heard a faint, funny little screech from the direction of the hedge. No one else seemed to have heard it and he was just beginning to think he'd imagined it when it came again. Looking up he saw Colin walking quietly into the field and sitting down in the shade of a tree where he could hardly be seen in the gloom. Just then Oliver called out that it was time to tidy up and go home.

"Jim, you know where the finds trays are kept. Please take the jewellery to the shed and the students can take the pottery. I'll lock up before I leave the site. Right everyone, make sure everything is tidy and I'll see you tomorrow. Well done, another successful day."

Jim carefully carried the heavy jewellery tray to the shed. Inside, where he couldn't be seen he carefully counted the finds before putting the tray on a shelf. There was one necklace, seven brooches, two bracelets and several buckles and hair pins. The students came in with the pottery tray and left quickly leaving Jim to look round carefully. He finally left the shed pulling the door closed behind him.

"You've taken your time," said Oliver who was walking over the field carrying a pile of trowels and gloves. "What on earth were you doing in there?"

Jim nearly told Oliver about the missing coins but then thought it would sound as if he were accusing Oliver of stealing them.

"Oh, I was just checking everything was alright he stammered nervously."

"Well why on earth wouldn't it be, boy?" laughed Oliver. "Off you go, see you tomorrow." He set back across the field looking for anything else to tidy away.

Jim walked back to his bag and looked around for Colin. Sure enough, he had moved away from the tree and was walking slowly and casually towards the shed. When he saw that the coast was clear, he opened the door just wide enough to squeeze in and pulled it closed behind him. In no time at all he was out again, his hands stuffed deep into his pockets and his curtain of hair hiding his face. He walked towards the gate and as he reached the lane his dad appeared and flinging his arm around Colin's shoulders he patted him on the back. The two of them walked off quickly down the lane and were gone.

"Did you see that?" hissed Jackie, sticking her head through the hedge. "What was he doing and why did his dad meet him like last night? I can't make head or tale of it."

"I can," thought Jim. "He took some coins last night and I bet he's just pinched some of the jewellery. I must tell Oliver." But even as he was thinking about it, he saw Oliver walking out of the gate, talking to Farmer Cooper who was being pulled along by two massive dogs.

"I'll tie these two here overnight," Farmer Cooper was saying. "If anyone comes into the field they'll bark loud enough to wake the dead and I'll be along in a jiffy."

It was too late. Oliver had locked the shed and was leaving and now two fierce looking dogs were guarding the place. Jim decided he would speak to Oliver in the morning.

Chapter Seven: Jim in Trouble

"Jackie or Jill?" Jim asked one of the twins as five children gathered once more at the farmer's gate, ready for another long day's hard work.

"Can't you really tell us apart? I'm Jill of course, we've had a change of plan and Jackie's coming in the afternoon," she giggled, thrilled that she and her sister could still confuse their friends.

"I hope nothing happened again here last night," Amelia said, "Farmer Cooper's dogs should've kept any vandals away."

Jim hoped so too, but he was more worried about the conversation he was planning to have with Oliver about Colin the thief. But as they walked through the gate into the field the children saw to their horror that the vandals had indeed been back. Once again the trenches had been filled in and equipment thrown around. Oliver was surveying the wreckage, a very grim look on his face.

"I can't understand it, those dogs were fierce enough to frighten anybody away and Farmer Cooper said he would hear them if they barked," he said in dismay. "He's already been to take them away and he can't understand why he didn't hear them. Come on everyone, we're back to square one, we have to clear this mess up before we can get any further with the dig."

Everyone groaned but got down to work eagerly, wanting to clear the site so they could see more of the ancient Roman villa they had discovered. All of them felt that the villa somehow belonged to them and they wanted to do their best for it.

"I can't believe anyone would do this to our villa," Laura said, close to tears.

"Some people want their heads examining," muttered Sameer darkly, obviously very upset.

Jim wanted to tell Oliver about his suspicions about the thefts from the finds shed as soon as possible. He still wasn't sure if Oliver had removed the coins but he was absolutely sure Colin had taken something last night. He looked at the group of older lads and there Colin was, doing nothing as usual, but leaning against a shovel grinning. Jim wondered if he was responsible for the vandalism as well.

He saw Oliver walking away from the finds shed and knew immediately that he had noticed something missing from the trays. Oliver hurried over to the other archaeologists and was soon deep in conversation with them. Jim followed, eager now to tell Oliver he knew who the thief was but to his astonishment when Oliver saw him he turned on him shouting,

"It's you lad, isn't it? You've taken coins and some of the jewellery from the shed, haven't you? Don't deny it! You took ages to get the finds tray for the jewellery yesterday and I bet you took the coins then. And last night you were hanging round the shed again. Well I want you off the dig immediately and if you don't return those finds by this evening I'm ringing the police!"

"But it wasn't me, I know who took them, it was………."

"Stop blaming someone else, I know it was you, so get out now before I call the police this minute!" yelled Oliver.

Anger and shame surged through Jim as he went to get his bag. Everyone had heard Oliver shouting at him and everyone stopped work and stared at him as he walked miserably off the field. The four children stood open mouthed with astonishment as Jim disappeared from sight.

"Jim would never steal anything!" Sameer said.

"What are we going to do?" asked Amelia, "We can't just let him be accused of something he didn't do. It's so unfair."

"Well we don't actually know he didn't take the stuff, do we?" said Laura. "Perhaps it was him after all."

"How dare you say that!" Sameer shouted. "That's an awful thing to say about Jim."

The children stared angrily at each other and Jill burst into tears.

"It's all gone wrong, what are we going to do?"

Just then Oliver appeared, "Come on kids, it'll be ok. I'm sure Jim didn't really mean any harm. He'll return the finds and then everything'll be alright. Come on; let's get all this mess tidied up. I wonder what you'll find today?" he smiled.

The children returned to work but the day had been spoilt. Although the sun still blazed from a bright blue, cloudless sky, everything seemed tinged with grey. No one was talking to Laura who went to work in another part of the field. In fact the children were very quiet and subdued which is why they heard the barn owl screeching sound from behind the hedge. Moving quietly to the edge of the field they found Jackie jumping up and down excitedly in the lane and next to her stood a miserable looking Jim.

"I know it was Colin who stole the jewellery," she said in a fierce whisper. "Last night I saw him hand it over to his dad here in the lane. I heard his dad say it was a fine bit of jewellery and should fetch a lot of money when they sold it. So I can prove it wasn't Jim, can't I?"

"Well it's only your word against theirs," said Amelia doubtfully. "Who will Oliver believe and how are you going to explain to him that half the time you are on the dig and half the time you are skulking around behind this hedge? It sounds suspicious and not very honest."

"Yes, Oliver is more likely to believe an older boy and his father than us," Sameer said gloomily.

"Leave it to us, we'll think up a plan, won't we?" Jackie whispered cheerfully to Jim who didn't look at all cheerful. "You lot get back to work and we'll tell you the plan when we've thought of it." With that, she and Jim disappeared from view leaving the children wondering doubtfully if there was any plan which could get Jim out of the mess he seemed to be in.

Once the vandalism had been tidied up digging began again, but the children didn't have the heart to work with enthusiasm. They had been given the job of sieving the soil from around the walls of the villa but they found nothing of interest. All they could think about was poor Jim and the unfairness of it all and wonder about what sort of plan Jackie would come up with. Laura had said she was sorry for what she had said and they'd agreed to forgive her.

"After all, we've got to stick together or we won't be able to help Jim at all," Amelia had said, and they all agreed.

It was the hottest day yet and the midday sun seemed intent on baking them alive.

"Ok folks," called Oliver, "we'll take an early lunch break today. It's so hot and I don't want anyone getting sunstroke. Make sure you all have enough to drink, and don't forget the sun cream. The children had been sensible about putting on sun cream and wearing their hats and sunglasses but they were all getting such a tan that when they took off their sunglasses their brown faces showed up the white skin around their eyes.

"You look like a panda only in reverse," laughed Jill to Amelia.

"Speak for yourself, you look as if you've been dragged through a hedge backwards," Amelia replied looking at Jill's smudged face and dishevelled hair.

There was no sign of Jackie and Jim behind the hedge and everyone wondered what they were doing and if they'd had any bright ideas.

"If they don't think of something soon the police will be here and Jim will be dragged off to jail," Jill said dramatically.

"Oh come on, it won't be that bad," Laura responded, "but it is serious. Any finds made on a dig belong to the landowner, so actually Colin has been stealing from Farmer Cooper, but how are we going to prove it?"

At that moment a screech came from the hedge and there were Jackie and Jim and this time Jim looked more hopeful.

"We've thought of a plan," Jackie whispered in excitement. We've just seen Colin's dad hanging around in the lane. Of course he doesn't know that Jim has been accused of stealing the finds, but of course Colin does know. He won't be able to steal anything from the finds tray in the shed because I'm sure Oliver will be taking extra care and will have it locked up all the time."

"So how does that help us?" Sameer asked doubtfully."

"Don't you see?" Jackie answered impatiently, "Colin's Dad is still expecting Colin to bring him something and so Colin will have to find it himself and put it straight in his pocket before anyone sees it."

"Oh yes," answered Laura," so instead of slipping away in the afternoon and only coming back at the end of the day to steal from the finds tray, he will have to stay all day and try to find something."

"Well, even if he does that, how's it going to help Jim?" Amelia asked, puzzled.

"Because you lot are going to watch him like a hawk and catch him red-handed!" Jackie squeaked in excitement.

"Gosh, yes," Sameer said excitedly. "Look, Colin's already back at work excavating that trench. Usually he slips off after lunch. You're right; it looks as though he's determined to find something himself. I've never seen him work so hard!"

Sure enough, there was Colin already scraping away while the rest of his friends lay back on the grass under the trees, their eyes closed, all seemingly asleep.

"Ok, so we don't take our eyes off Colin this afternoon," announced Jill. "The first one to see him do anything suspicious alerts the rest of us and we'll all surround him in case he tries to make a run for it. Let's swap places now Jackie. I'll keep Jim company in the lane and keep an eye on Colin's dad."

There was much rustling and rattling of leaves as the twins pushed their way in opposite directions through the hedge. The others could only tell the difference between them because the newly arrived Jackie was still clean and not red in the face from working in the sun all morning.

"Back to work then," announced Sameer, "and keep your eyes peeled; we're all on thief watch!"

Chapter Eight: Gotcha!

Fortunately the four children were assigned jobs where they could all keep Colin in sight.

"It's a good job we're not at the bottom of a trench or we wouldn't see anything," said Laura as she shovelled soil into a sieve for Amelia to shake and rattle, but to no avail. Finds seemed hard to come by today.

"It's such hard work," complained Amelia. "My arms are killing me and it makes it so much harder that I have to keep on turning round to watch Colin. It's making my neck stiff and sore too."

Jackie and Sameer weren't finding it any easier either. They were down on their hands and knees scraping away the soil from the top of a wall with their trowels. They had to keep swivelling round and lifting their heads up to keep Colin in sight and their backs and necks were twisted and painful. It was funny that now they had lost all interest in finding artefacts themselves and were desperate for Colin to make a find so he could steal it and they could catch him.

The afternoon wore on, the sun was relentless, the air shimmered and danced, flies landed on their sweaty faces. All that could be heard was the scraping of trowels, the sifting of soil and the scuffling of the workers as they moved around. To make matters worse, the children could hardly bear the suspense. Would Colin make a find? Would he hide it in his pocket? Would they see him do it? Would they have the courage to accuse him of theft? Would Oliver believe them? What if Colin thought up a good excuse? What would Colin's dad do? All these questions and many more swirled round in their hot, sweaty, anxious heads. It was almost unbearable.

And then it happened! Sameer saw Colin lift something from the soil, give it a quick rub, look around the field and then shove it in his pocket. Sameer leapt up with a shout and ran towards Colin, the others following close behind. Before he knew what was going on, Colin was surrounded by four children, all jumping up and down and shouting. Jackie gave a loud barn owl screech and Jim popped his head up over the hedge.

"Whatever's going on?" shouted Oliver as he stormed towards them. All work stopped as everyone stood and stared at the commotion being made by four small children.

"It's Colin; he's found something and put it in his pocket," Sameer said excitedly, "I saw him with my own eyes!"

What are you talking about?" asked Oliver gruffly. "We've already found our thief, him over there," he said pointing to Jim who was just arriving at the scene. "And what are you doing here anyway? I told you to get off the site until you brought back what you've stolen. Have you brought it back?"

"No Sir, Jim answered breathlessly. "It wasn't me who stole the coins and jewellery; it was me who discovered they'd gone from the shed. I was going to tell you this morning but you accused me before I had chance to explain."

"Yes, said Laura, "we think it was Colin here who took the artefacts and gave them to his dad to be sold. So we watched him this afternoon and Sameer just saw him put something in his pocket."

At that moment Colin made a dash for it, pushing Amelia over and running for the gate.

"Not so fast my lad," growled Oliver who moved as quickly as lightning and grabbed Colin by his collar. "Let's see if what these kids are saying is true. Let's see what you've got. Come on then, empty your pockets."

Colin's face couldn't be seen behind the curtain of dark hair, but he shrugged and putting his hand into his pocket pulled something out.

"Hand it over then lad," Oliver said grimly. Colin put the object on Oliver's outstretched hand and everyone gasped. It was a little statue of a woman, and even though it was covered in soil they could see it was beautiful. In silence Oliver fished out his little brush and bottle of water and carefully cleaned off the dirt until they could all see that there, lying on his hand was a lovely figurine, its delicate form a greenish colour, gleaming and winking at them in the sunlight.

"Well," Oliver said, "you've made the best find yet! This is a figurine of a Roman goddess in bronze, probably Minerva or Venus and it's really quite rare. And to think you were going to steal it." He turned angrily on Colin. "And did you steal the coins and the jewellery too? Are you our thief?"

Colin's shoulders drooped. "Yeh, it was me," he admitted. It was my dad. He wanted me to take what I could so he could sell it. It's his

162

job see, selling stolen stuff. 'S'not my fault, I was just helping him do his job."

Before anyone could say anything else there was a girl's scream and an angry yell from behind the hedge.

"Help me, I've got him!" called a voice which the children knew was Jill's. "Hurry up, I can't hold him much longer. Quick, I've got Colin's dad!"

"I'll stay here with this boy and call the police," shouted Oliver. "Quick, some of you; go and get the dad.

Archaeologists and students alike raced through the gate and into the lane, the children with them. An amazing sight met their eyes. Colin's dad was lying sprawled on the ground, his feet tangled up in a mesh of string. Jill was bouncing up and down on his back, hitting him on the head with a branch every time he tried to get up.

"Jackie and Jim set a booby trap for him this morning!" she yelled triumphantly. "We knew he'd be along here to get the loot that Colin stole, so we stretched this string all across the lane and sure enough, when he heard the fuss from the field he hurried along to see what was happening and didn't notice the string. He tripped over and fell to the ground and I jumped on top of him. But hurry up; I can't hold him much longer."

Colin's dad was still struggling as he was hauled to his feet and disentangled from the string.

"Blooming kids," he snarled. "Why don't you just mind your own business? Keep your horrible little noses out of my affairs."

"I'm afraid it's too late for that," one of the archaeologists said, grabbing his arms and pulling them behind his back. "Here are the police."

Sirens wailing, two police cars screeched to a halt by the gate and four policemen leapt out. Colin's dad was dragged down the lane towards the cars and was met by his son who was being pulled out of the field by Oliver.

"These are our two thieves, officers," Oliver said. "I will be down to the police station to press charges as quickly as possible. But first I have a few matters to settle."

As the police cars reversed and drove back down the lane with their scowling occupants hunched between burly police men, Oliver led everyone back onto the field.

"Back to work everyone, we have an hour before we finish for the day. I want to talk to these incredible children. Come over here kids."

Gathering round Oliver, the children could hardly contain their excitement. They were heroes! They had caught two thieves! And Jim was safe! They took it in turns to explain their part in all that had happened and Jim had the biggest say of all. Although he was the biggest hero of them all, he had narrowly missed being taken off in a police car himself! Oliver listened carefully, asked lots of questions and breathed a sigh of relief.

"Thank goodness you're such bright, clever, honest kids," he said. "I can never thank you enough for saving those valuable artefacts and finding the thieves. And most of all," he said turning to Jim, "I owe you a huge apology. I falsely accused you of being a thief and for that I am very sorry. And so when we do the re-enactment and you all get dressed up for the film, I want you to be the owner of our villa, a wealthy landowner and farmer, a proud British-Roman citizen!"

"Oh gosh, thank you," Jim gasped. "That's fantastic. I'll enjoy being rich and powerful! So, you slaves," he laughed turning to the others, "as you helped me when I was in trouble, I won't work you too hard when I'm your master!"

"Oh thank you, sir," Jackie curtsied towards Jim and everyone laughed.

"Come on," said Oliver, "time for you lot to go home, both slaves and master. The rest of us will finish off and clear up. Farmer Cooper will bring his dogs again and we might get the police to pop by too. I'm hoping we'll get the finds back from Colin's dad; I don't think he'll have had time to sell them on yet. So see you in the morning, and once again, a huge thank you."

The children hurried to get their bags and set off towards home. They were very tired but very happy.

"I wonder if the vandals will come again tonight," said Jill.

"Probably not, I bet they were Colin and his dad," answered Amelia.

"Let's hope so," Jim said, "but I'm not so sure. I've got a plan," he added mysteriously.

"Not another one!" laughed Laura, "I've had enough excitement to last me a life time! Come on Amelia. We'll see you tomorrow."

With that the children went their separate ways, looking forward to a long shower, clean clothes and a big tea.

Chapter Nine: Night Adventures

Jim, the twins and Sameer walked home slowly.

"Well, what are you thinking, Jim?" asked Jackie. "Come on, spill the beans."

"I'm sure Colin and his dad weren't the vandals," Jim answered thoughtfully. "They were just after valuables to sell. The person who made all the mess must have another motive. They obviously want to slow the dig down to make it last longer."

"Yes, and that wouldn't be Farmer Cooper; he wants us off his land as quickly as possible. So who could it be?" wondered Sameer.

"Well let's find out tonight. Let's go and see who it is," Jim replied.

"Gosh, that's very daring," Jill said, "what's the plan?"

"That is the plan," answered Jim, "we keep watch and find out who it is when he arrives."

"That's no plan," said Sameer. "What about the dogs? They'll bark when they see us and then Farmer Cooper will come along, find us there and think we're the vandals."

"Well of course we'll stay well away, out of sight of the dogs," Jim said scornfully, "I'm not that daft."

"We'll have to wear dark clothes so we won't be seen," said Jackie, warming to the idea.

"Yes, and one of us should have a mobile with them so we can call for help if things go wrong," suggested Jill.

"Right, it'll just be the four of us," Jim said, "no need to tell anyone else."

"But how will we get away from home without our parents knowing? We'll have to go out quite early in case we miss the vandal's arrival, but then our parents will still be up and will hear us going out," Sameer asked doubtfully.

"Now I really have got a plan," laughed Jackie excitedly. "In the summer our parents sometimes let us camp out in the garden at night. We've got two little tents; we could sleep in one and you two boys in the other. Then we can slip out of the garden and back again without anyone knowing."

"You're a genius," shouted Jim, slapping Jackie on the back. "All we've got to do is ask our parents and I'm sure mine will say yes; what about you Sameer?"

"If I tell them I'll be with you I'm sure they'll agree," Sameer said enthusiastically.

"Right, you two, be in our back garden by seven o'clock. Bring your sleeping bags and pyjamas and we'll pretend to go to bed and then wait until it's dark before we go to the field," Jackie said. "See you soon!"

Just before seven o'clock Jim met Sameer at his garden gate and they hurried along to the twins'. Their back garden was long and at the bottom of it, as far away as possible from the house two little igloo shaped tents were pitched under the trees. Jackie and Jill were there and like the boys, were already dressed in dark clothes over their pyjamas. Their Mum was there too and greeted the boys cheerfully.

"What fun," she laughed. "I've made you all a picnic supper which you can have before you go to bed and perhaps you can skip teeth cleaning for one night. It'll be dark by about nine o'clock and I think you should be in your sleeping bags by then. Sleep well, don't get into any mischief and I'll see you in the morning."

The children played in the garden, tucked into their bed time picnic and when dusk started to fall they made their plans.

"If we go the back way to Cooper's farm no one will see us," suggested Jackie.

"And where do you think we should hide when we get there?" asked Sameer. "We don't want those dogs to see us, but we do want a good view of the field."

"I think just by the gate into the field," said Jim. "We can climb onto the fence and see what's going on, the dogs won't see us and we can make a quick getaway if we have to."

"If we spread out along the fence there'll be a better chance of one of us seeing something," said Jackie. "I'll use my barn owl screech as a sign that we should all run away if something goes wrong," she added.

"What do we do if we actually see someone there?" Jill asked anxiously. She was beginning to get cold feet about the whole venture.

"Well of course we phone the police on your mobile, you did say you were bringing it, didn't you, Jill?" asked Jim. There was a long pause in which the three children stared at Jill.

"No, it's at home," she stammered, "I only suggested that we took one with us; I thought someone else would bring theirs."

"Well that's great," Jackie hissed at her sister angrily, "and that means we have no torch either, I thought we would use the one on your phone; you're just so stupid!"

"Don't blame me, Jill sobbed, "why didn't someone else bring a phone and a torch, it wasn't just up to me, it's not fair. I'm going back to the house and good luck with your stupid plan."

"Come back," called Sameer, "you're right, it's not just your fault."

But Jill had disappeared into the darkening night leaving the other three to carry out the plan without her.

"We'd better hurry up in case she tells Mum and Dad where we're going," said Jackie jumping up quickly. "Come on, before they come out to stop us."

Before the boys could stop her she had flounced out of the garden towards the back lane and they hurried after her. As they left the village they realised how dark it was. None of them had realised how absolutely pitch black it was going to be away from the street lights.

The night sky was totally black without stars or moon and the warm night air seemed to wrap them round like a blanket muffling any sound. Jackie didn't seem to mind the darkness and raced silently on in front of the boys avoiding any obstacle in her path. The boys didn't have such good night vision and tried desperately to keep up with her. It wasn't long before Jim crashed into a low wall sending him sprawling onto the ground and soon after Sameer bashed into an overhanging tree branch, nearly knocking him senseless. They didn't dare call Jackie in case they were heard but eventually, realising they weren't close behind her she slowed down and waited for them to catch up.

"Hurry up, slow coaches," she said impatiently.

"Have you got infrared vision or something?" groaned Jim, rubbing his bruised shins. "Slow down, we ordinary mortals can't keep up with you."

"Just follow close behind me," said Jackie," we're nearly there."

Sure enough, the boys could just make out the gate into the field and the fence next to it. In the farmyard in front of the gate stood the huge yellow digger, parked there in case it was needed again. The gate was closed and all was quiet, except for the faint rustle of leaves in the nearby trees.

"Good, no one seems to be here yet," whispered Jim. "Let's hide near the fence under the trees. Anybody coming won't see us in our dark clothes, especially as they won't be expecting us to be here."

Jackie stood on the top rung of the fence and peered into the field. Now that her eyes had got used to the dark she could see the dark shapes of the soil heaps, the shed and then the moving shapes of the two tethered dogs as they roamed back and forth, but nothing else. The children settled down to wait in the warm stillness of the night. Suddenly there was a flurry of air above their heads and they saw dark shapes swooping and swirling above them. Jackie let out a small shriek and covered her head with her hands.

"Ugh, bats," she shivered, "they might fly into my hair, I couldn't bear it."

"Of course they won't," said Jim, "they've been out hunting for insects and are flying back to roost in the trees and their radar makes them even better in the dark than you are!"

They were so entertained watching the flock of little creatures flying back to the trees that at first they didn't hear the approaching car. It was Sameer who first saw the two beams of light cutting through the darkness. Crouching down at the base of the fence they watched as the car stopped and the driver got out and opened the gate. He drove the car a little way into the field and then left it with the engine running and the headlights shining out, illuminating the whole field. Knowing that the glare of the lights would prevent the man from seeing them, the children climbed to the top of the fence and watched as he walked towards the dogs. Instead of growling and barking the dogs ran up to the man, their tails wagging. He bent down to stroke them, ruffling their fur and pulling their ears.

"Gosh," whispered Jim, "they know him."

"Of course, it must be Jed Cooper, the farmer's son," Jackie answered. "They're his dogs; they will have known him all their lives so that's why they're not barking. But what's he doing here? I thought he had left home."

Just then, Jed, if that was who it was, picked up a spade and started to shovel soil into the excavated trenches. He worked fast and furiously and soon the trenches were filled in. Then he started to throw spades and brushes in all directions and kick angrily at wheel barrows and even the door of the shed.

"What are we going to do?" Jackie asked in a panic. Everything had happened so fast that they had just stood and watched the furious man in astonishment.

"Look he's coming back. We've got to stop him getting away, but how?" asked Jim.

"I know," cried Sameer, and before they could stop him he was racing towards the digger. In no time at all he had clambered into the cab and was fiddling with the controls. Suddenly the engine leapt into life with a deep growl and the huge machine lurched backwards, its bucket swinging around wildly. There was a crunch of levers and the digger started to roll forward on its caterpillar treads. Slowly at first and then faster, the machine juddered towards the gate and the parked car.

"He's going to try and park behind the car and block it in," said Jim excitedly.

They watched the small figure of Sameer as he wrestled with the controls. A look of panic was on his face and they realised that the digger was out of control. If he didn't stop the machine soon it would crush the car. They heard a shout behind them and turning, saw Jed racing towards them across the field. He had a shovel in his hand and was waving it wildly in the air. Trapped between him and the runaway digger, Jim and Jackie froze in horror. Just before Jed reached them the digger came to a sudden grinding halt inches from the car and the engine cut out. At that moment Jim heard the screech of a barn owl and wasting no time raced off past the car and machine. Seeing him run, Sameer leapt from the cab and followed him. Tripping over some things and crashing into others they made their escape down the lane as if their lives depended on it. Only when they were half way to the twins' house did they stop to catch their breath. Panting and gasping they looked round for Jackie, but she wasn't there. Then from out of the pitch black sky a ghostly white shape floated towards them and then over them towards the trees. As they watched the beautiful creature float away they heard the sharp screech of the barn owl and an answering call from the trees. A sudden awful realisation hit Jim. Back at the field he hadn't heard Jackie's signal for them to run away, he had heard a real barn owl. That meant that Jackie must still be there, alone with Jed, the furious, raving vandal.

"Quick, we've got to go back and rescue Jackie," he called to an astonished Sameer. "We've left her there with that mad man."

Just then the boys heard shouts and saw the beams of three torches approaching them down the lane. Jill was in the lead and her parents were following close behind.

"Where's Jackie?" asked Jill, "she should be with you."

Speechless, Jim gestured towards the field and the five of them hurried down the lane, dreading what they would find round the corner.

When they reached the field an extraordinary sight met their eyes. The car was still there in the gateway and the digger was still where it had come to rest, inches from the car. But to their astonishment in the light of the headlamps they could see Jackie and the man sitting on the grass together and laughing. Two huge dogs were lying beside them having their ears fondled and their tummies tickled.

"It's all ok," said Jackie as she saw everyone approaching. "Jed here is great. He doesn't want his dad to build cottages in the field. He wants everyone to be able to see all the Roman remains here and is worried his dad might have the villa destroyed to make way for the new buildings. He wasn't trying to ruin the dig; he was trying to protect it by slowing everything down to give his dad time to change his mind."

"It probably wasn't the cleverest plan in the world," admitted Jed, "but it was the only thing I could think of doing."

"Well I don't know about all that," said the twins' mum. "All I know is that it's nearly midnight and my daughters are running around the countryside when they should be tucked up in bed. It's too late now, but we'll be having a serious talk in the morning. Come on everyone, home time. You boys may as well sleep in the garden; it's too late to go home now."

Chapter Ten: Apologies and Explanations

The children were up bright and early even after their night's adventure. None of them seemed to be any the worse for wear and all were eager to get to the dig to see what was happening there.

"We'd better hurry up," said Jim impatiently, "otherwise Oliver might not let us back on the dig and we need to explain what happened last night."

"And I've got some explaining to do," said Sameer in a worried voice, "I've got to tell Oliver all about the digger." He shuddered at the thought of how close he had been to squashing Jed's car with the out of control machine.

"Oliver probably already knows everything," Jackie replied. "Last night Jed promised to talk to him in the morning to explain why he wrecked the dig and how we tried to stop him."

"Well let's go and find out," Jill said.

"Not so soon you lot," called the twins' Mum as they were preparing to set off after breakfast. "I've made a packed lunch for each of you and now it's time for the serious talk I promised you last night!"

After a good talking to she let them go and they hurried through the village.

"I wonder what Oliver will say to Jed," Sameer said, "and what Farmer Cooper will do when he knows that Jed has come back?"

"Well he's not going to be at all happy that Jed wrecked the dig and slowed it down," Jim said, "all he wants to do is get those holiday cottages built."

Arriving on the field, the children were pleased to see the digger was back in its place and the whole site had been tidied up. There was no sign of last night's events apart from the marks of caterpillar treads in the dust by the gate and Jed's car which was now parked neatly in the farmyard.

Oliver saw the children standing hesitantly by the gate wondering if they were welcome back on the dig. He hurried over and before any of them could speak was giving each of them bear hugs and handshakes.

"Well done, very well done," he beamed. "Jed has told me all about last night and how you came to stop him. Very brave of you, very brave indeed. And I believe you're quite an expert on the digger," he turned to Sameer, smiling and winking. "I can't thank you all enough for your help. It was you who found our thief yesterday and if you hadn't found Jed last night we wouldn't have him helping us here now." The children turned round and were thrilled to see Jed on his hands and knees scraping away the soil covering the mosaic floor. He waved cheerfully when he saw them and then returned to work.

"Jed went back to the farmhouse last night after you had gone home and had a long talk with his dad," Oliver continued. "They have made up their differences and Farmer Cooper has changed his mind about the dig and is happy for it to carry on. I think it might be something to do with Jed telling him that any finds we make will belong to him! So we can carry on now with nothing to worry about; no thieves, no vandals and no angry farmers to contend with! So off you go back to work; your two little friends have been wondering where you are."

They found Amelia and Laura digging out a trench near one of the walls.

"Where've you lot been?" complained Laura. "We've been slaving away for an hour already and you're only just rolling up!"

"It's a long story," laughed Jill, "they can tell you all about it; I'm off home until this afternoon." With that she slipped off through the hedge.

"What beats me is that Oliver never seems to notice if there's one or two of you here at a time," Jim said to Jackie as he watched Jill disappear.

"Never mind about them," Amelia said impatiently, "we want to know what you were all up to last night."

So as they scraped, dug and sieved they told the astonished girls about the events of the previous night, how Jed was now helping and how farmer Cooper was happy about the dig and was looking forward to keeping the finds they discovered on his land.

"Well I wish you'd told me what you were going to do," Amelia said, "I would have joined you. It's not fair me missing out on all the fun."

"Don't be silly, Amelia," snapped Laura, "it doesn't sound at all like fun to me, more like a stupid prank. Just be grateful you weren't involved; you don't know what might have happened."

"Oh stop arguing you two," said Jim. "Let's just get on with the digging and see what else we can find!"

The morning wore on, the sun grew hotter and hotter, sweat trickled down their backs, hands ached, knees hurt and frustration grew as no new finds were made. Just as they were about to give up Oliver called them to stop for lunch.

"After lunch I'll be giving you all an official up-to-date report on the progress of the dig," he announced.

After eating their picnic, the children relaxed under the trees with their eyes closed. The warmth of the air, the sweet smell of grass and hot earth and the buzz and rustle of insects almost lulled them to sleep.

"Wake up lazybones," shrilled an excited voice. "Look who I've found!"

Jill stood above them and squinting through half closed eyes they saw another familiar figure.

"Ali!" shouted Jim, "you're back from your holiday!"

Everyone sat up and there was Ali grinning down at them all.

"Well you lot seem to have been having some exciting times while I've been away," he said, " Jill's told me all about it. I wish I'd been here too."

"Well never mind, you're here now," said Sameer jumping up and bashing Ali on the back. "Are you going to ask Oliver if you can come and help here tomorrow?"

"We've already asked him," Jill said importantly, "and he said yes."

"You don't know what you're letting yourself in for!" groaned Jackie, "I've had enough today. I'm off home now, see you later everybody, come on Ali."

No sooner had they disappeared through the hedge than Oliver was calling them all to gather round.

Chapter Eleven: A Change of Plan

"I have some rather surprising news," Oliver told everyone as they gathered round him. "Although our dig has been a great success and we have found a Roman villa belonging to a farmer who lived nearly two thousand years ago, the University has decided to close the dig down at the end of the week. By then we will have uncovered all the walls and worked out the size and shape of the buildings and hopefully have found more artefacts. The University will return next summer to continue the excavation. Farmer Cooper has agreed to build his cottages in the next field so this site will be preserved as a place of historical interest. So I'm afraid we only have two days left here."

"But what about the re-enactment and the filming?" asked one of the students.

"Oh don't worry about that," laughed Oliver, "you'll all get your moment of fame. We will be filming the day after the dig has finished and I believe a television channel may want to use it for a schools' programme on the Romans. You kids might even be watching yourselves on telly! So time is short, let's see what else we can discover here before we have to leave. Back to work everyone."

"I can't say I'm sorry we've only got two more days left after this," Amelia said as she sieved soil; "it's been jolly hard work."

Although they didn't want to admit it, the others felt the same.

"Yes, you can have too much of a good thing," Jim said. "I must say I'm looking forward to all of us playing back in Fern Valley again."

The day finished with another find of brooches and a bracelet in one trench and some more coins in another. The mosaic floor was almost completely uncovered and everyone admired the beautiful colours and patterns which had lasted so long under the soil in a farmer's field.

"A good end to a good day," Oliver said. "Come on everyone, home time." They all downed tools, tidied up the site and left, looking forward to the last two days' work.

The next day, seven eager children arrived for a hard day's work. Jackie and Jill had decided they would both work all day for the last two days and enjoyed the fact that Oliver had never noticed their little tricks. Ali was keen to get started and Oliver put him to work with Jim and Sameer in the last trench which had been dug.

"This trench should show us where the kitchen was," Oliver said, "so expect to find lots of pottery! Be careful to do what the student tells you."

Knowing there were only two days left, and with the film in mind, the children worked with enthusiasm. Laura and Amelia were given the easy job of holding a measuring stick against the excavated walls whilst the archaeologists measured and recorded their dimensions and then took photographs. Meanwhile Jackie, Jim and Jill sieved soil and then loaded it into wheelbarrows and pushed it out of sight, ready for the filming.

"We've got the hardest job by far," gasped Jill, "I'm beginning to regret working all day."

"Me too," her sister replied, "but it'll be worth it to be actors in the re-enactment. I've always wanted to be a film star."

"It's hardly Hollywood," smiled Jim, "but I expect it'll be worth it as long as we don't die of heat exhaustion first."

Although it didn't seem possible, it was even hotter than the day before. The TV and radio were talking about the longest heat wave for twenty years with record temperatures. The grass in the field was becoming yellow and the soil was turning to dust which flew up into their faces as they scraped, dug and sieved it. Oliver called an early lunch and said they could have twenty minutes longer than usual. There was no birdsong and the field was quiet and still as everyone gratefully lay down under the trees to rest. So when Tom bounded into the field with a cheery hello, everyone was startled. He had been the first of the Fern Valley Venturers and with Ali had built the tree house which they all loved to play in. The children had missed him and were pleased to see him back from his holidays.

"I asked the man if I could come and help you tomorrow," he said cheerily. "And he said yes. I've got to look after my little sister this afternoon but I'll be along tomorrow morning."

"That means you'll only be working one day," said Laura, "we've been here all week."

"Think yourself lucky," laughed Jim, "it's been jolly hard work but we've sort of enjoyed it."

"I'd better be going home," Tom said, "it's good to be back, see you all tomorrow."

Lunchtime was over too soon and the afternoon dragged on terribly. There was one bright spot when Sameer found an interesting piece of metalwork in the kitchen area and then the student managed to dig out a second complete and undamaged pot. Oliver was very pleased and said the pot was just the sort which was being used in the time of Emperor Julian whose head was on the coins they'd found before.

Just before five o'clock Oliver called a halt. "I want you all here ready to work hard tomorrow," he said. "We'll need to complete one or two trenches and then clean and tidy everything up ready for the re-enactment of A Day in the Life of a Romano- British Farmer and his Family. Obviously we don't want anything modern like wheelbarrows or plastic bottles to get into the film so we have to clear everything away. Off you go, see you all tomorrow."

Chapter Twelve: Outrageous!

The last day of the dig saw all eight Fern Valley Venturers arriving bright and early. They were all excited to be together and were keen to get the site ready for the filming. As it was his first day, Tom didn't really know how to do anything useful and everyone was too busy to show him. Ali wasn't much more help and so the two of them hovered around the edge of things, not putting in a lot of effort. The other children worked long and hard and took even shorter breaks than usual. They wanted to get the site just how Oliver wanted it to be and they were longing to know which part each of them would be playing in the film. They all knew that Jim was going to be the owner of the villa just as Oliver had promised him after he had caught Colin the thief but they wondered who the others would play.

"Knowing our luck we'll be a couple of slaves," laughed Jackie.

"Yes we'll probably be running round after you all day, Jim, cooking your meals and cleaning your villa," agreed Jill.

"Oh I hope I am the lady of the house so I can wear a beautiful tunic with a cloak fastened with a brooch like the ones we found," Laura sighed.

"I don't care who I am," Sameer said, "as long as I'm not your son, Jim," he laughed.

There was a surprise visit from Farmer Cooper who came to look at the Roman villa which had suddenly appeared in his field.

"Well I never, who would have thought it? And to think it was my son who discovered it," he said proudly patting Jed on the back.

"Well, he's changed his tune," Amelia said; "he was so against it before."

"Like Oliver said, I think it might be because all the finds we've made belong to him as the landowner," Jim said. "It might make him quite rich."

The long day's work was coming to an end and the hot, dusty, sticky children were waiting for the reward Oliver had promised them at the beginning of the week. They gathered round as Oliver announced their parts in the re-enactment.

"As I promised Jim, he will be the farmer and I have chosen Amelia to be his wife. The twins will be their daughters and I do hope they will both stay for the whole time," he said with a twinkle in his eye. "No appearing and disappearing through the hedge please!"

The twins blushed as they realised Oliver had known about their trick all the time.

"I want Laura to be the housekeeper, and Sameer to be the cook, both of them slaves."

Laura opened her mouth to protest but realised that Oliver would not change his mind. The children started to chatter among themselves until Oliver interrupted.

"Hang on, I haven't finished yet. I want Tom to be Jim and Amelia's son, the one who will inherit the farm, and Ali to be the steward, the one in charge of all the slaves and farm labourers."

Everyone gasped and then there was silence until Laura burst out, "But that's not fair, we've been here all week and Ali has only worked one day and Tom hardly at all. Why should they have parts?"

"Yes, every day we dug and scraped and sieved and shovelled for you but they've hardly done anything," Amelia said.

"If it hadn't been for Jim you'd never have found who was stealing the finds," Sameer said, "and what about him and the others discovering it was Jed who was the vandal?"

"You promised us that we would have parts in your play," said Jackie, "it's just not fair."

"Hold on a minute," Oliver said, "I *have* given you parts in my play, just as I promised. That was what I promised you at the beginning of the week and that's what I've given you. I'm very grateful for all you've done and you've got your promised payment."

"But what about Tom and Ali?" Jim asked.

"Well that's up to me. If I choose to give them the same as you even though they've worked less, that's my choice. It doesn't harm you, you've got everything I promised. I can be as generous as I like.

"But it's still not fair," Jill said.

"But aren't you pleased your friends are going to be in the play too? Aren't you happy that they've got the reward too? Would you rather that they missed out and just had to stand and watch you enjoy yourselves? Come on, be pleased for them. It's going to happen whether you like it or not!"

"It's absolutely outrageous," Laura said indignantly. "Absolutely outrageous!"

"It is, isn't it?" laughed Oliver. "Absolutely, incredibly and ridiculously outrageous! Come on then, let's get rehearsing."

And so it was that, whether they deserved it or not, eight Fern Valley Venturers appeared in a film called, "A day in the life of a Romano-British Farmer and his Family". They dressed up, acted their parts and walked around the villa they had helped to excavate that long hot summer's week. They played their parts splendidly and enjoyed every minute of it.

"Well done!" laughed Oliver. "Well done all of you!"

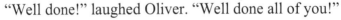

Can you tell that The Villa is a modern retelling of The Parable of the Workers in the Vineyard?

Check out Matthew 20 verses 1-16 in the Bible to see what you think.

The hidden meaning of the parable is that whenever, however and wherever we find God's love for us, he treats us all the same and loves us equally.

*Do you want to find and enjoy God's love for you now, or miss out by waiting until you get old?

The Verdict

Chapter One: Autumn Action

"Gosh, I can't believe it's dark already!" exclaimed Jill as she and Jackie burst out through the school doors into the playground.

"It's positively pitch black," agreed her sister as they headed towards home, "and it's jolly cold too," she shivered.

"Mum told you to take your coat this morning," Jill said, snuggling into her warm duffel coat and pulling up her hood. "I'm fine."

"Well how was I to know that by the time we came out of chess club we'd be living in the Arctic?" Jackie grumbled. "You needn't look so pleased with yourself; you've just stepped in an enormous puddle."

"Well I realise that," snapped Jill. "I'm the one with the wet foot."

"Hey you lot, wait for us!" The twins' argument was interrupted by their friends Laura and Amelia racing up behind them.

"What time are you two getting here tomorrow morning?" Laura asked. "We're setting up our stall at nine o'clock."

"So are we," replied Jill excitedly; "we want to sell everything we've made and get as much money as possible."

It was a Friday evening in October and the girls were talking about the school Autumn Fair which was being held in the hall the next day. There was a fair every year but this one was special. They were raising money for Heather House which was a place where very sick children could go with their families for short holidays. A boy in Year Six had a sister who had been very ill there, so the school had decided that all the money raised at the Fair and Bonfire Night would go to help Heather House build a special new playroom.

"We've been making sweets and chocolates for weeks now," Jill said, "and we've put them in little boxes with pretty paper so I'm sure we'll sell them all and make loads of money."

"Yes, the freezer is full of all the cakes we've made; there are boxes and boxes of them," laughed Amelia.

"I think our class will win the prize for raising the most money," added Jackie. "Jim and Ali have got their Good as New Toy stall and Sameer and Tom are running the Guess How Many Marbles in the Jar stall and there are lots of other stalls. It's like another Fern Valley Venturers Venture; all of us involved and working together."

"The last time we did that was on the dig at the Villa in the summer," Jill reminded them.

"Yes that was jolly hard work except for Tom and Ali who only turned up at the last minute," remembered Amelia.

"Well I think the Fair and Bonfire Night are going to be hard work too," commented Laura, "and I can't believe Mr Jones has put me in charge of looking after all the class's money until the end of the Fair."

"Well the Head knows you're pretty sensible," Amelia said, "so I suppose that's why he's chosen you."

"Yes, no running off on holiday with it," laughed Jackie. "Heather House needs all the money it can get!"

"Of course not," Laura said huffily. "Everyone knows I'm the best at maths in class. I'll add it all up and give it to Mr Jones at the end of the day, and not a penny will be missing!"

"Ok, keep your hair on," Jill laughed, "we're just kidding!"

"Yes, but it's true, you do have to be careful," warned Amelia. "Remember Mr Jones telling us about the money which mysteriously disappeared from the school office last week? He thinks there's a thief about the place and the Fair would be a perfect chance for him to strike again."

"He'd be a real low life to steal money from Heather House," remarked Jill.

"Well, I'm going to be extra careful so there'll be no chance of anyone stealing anything," Laura said confidently, "Mr Jones can rely on me."

"Come on, let's get home before we freeze to death," shivered Jackie, "and you don't want to get frostbite in that wet foot, Jill! See you tomorrow bright and early."

The girls hurried off home, eager to make their last minute preparations for The Grand Autumn Fair.

Chapter Two: The Grand Autumn Fair

By ten o'clock the next morning the school hall was packed with children and their parents milling around the array of stalls. Stalls lined the corridors too and some of the livelier games were out in the playground. Tom and Sameer were doing brisk business at their stand. Everyone seemed to think they knew how many marbles were in the jar and were keen to spend fifty pence to prove it. The boys wrote down everyone's name and their estimate and would announce the person who was nearest at the end of the day.

"Really, some people haven't got a clue," giggled Tom as he wrote down "one million" next to one boy's name.

"It doesn't matter," smiled Sameer, "as long as everyone here has a go and pays us fifty pence each, I reckon we could earn £100 just on this stall alone! I wonder if anyone will guess there are 1010 marbles in the jar?"

Just at that moment Laura appeared with her cash box.

"Count your money and give it me," she said importantly, "I'll make a note of it and let you know how much money you've made by the end of the day. I'm keeping it all safely locked in this tin."

The boys counted their takings and handed them over. Laura wrote the amount in her notebook, put the money in the cash box and moved on to the next stall.

"It's all very well her locking the box," Sameer said, "but what if the whole tin is stolen?"

"I don't think Laura will be letting it out of her grasp," grinned Tom. "She's taking her job very seriously."

Amelia's stall was besieged by people. The homemade cupcakes, tray bakes, chocolate krispies, lemon-drizzle cakes and Victoria sponges really were selling like hot cakes and she could hardly keep up with all her customers. Jill and Jackie were doing a roaring trade too with their home made sweets. Only Jim and Ali's second hand toy stall was quiet but that was because they had already sold the best stuff. The sad looking teddy bear and the battered box of Hungry Hippos would probably have to be reduced in price if they were going to sell them.

"Now that it's quieter, let's take it in turns to go round all the stalls," suggested Jim. "I want to buy some of Jill's sweets and then have a go at throwing the wet sponge at Mr Saunders." Sameer agreed and with his mouth full of Jill's delicious orange swirls, Jim was soon taking aim at the Year Six teacher. Mr Saunders was dressed in a bright orange wetsuit and matching orange wellies and looked pretty miserable. He held a large black umbrella in front of him to ward off the soaking sponges, but a surprising number seemed to get past it and hit him soggily in the face. Jim didn't take pity on him and enjoyed seeing Mr Saunders shudder as his sponge hit the mark.

"That's the best fifty pence I've spent in a long time," smiled Jim to himself. He'd never really liked Mr Saunders since he'd made him pick up litter all around the school after he'd once dropped a biscuit wrapper on the ground.

Meanwhile, Jackie had left Jill on the sweet stall and was having a go at the Wire Buzzer. Very carefully she threaded a loop of wire along a stretch of wire trying not to let it touch it and trigger the buzzer. But she was too quick and impatient and much to her annoyance kept on setting off the loud buzzer and the bright red flashing light. After several goes she gave up and watched in amazement as Tom managed to do it four times and win a big bag of popcorn.

"Never mind," laughed Tom, offering her some popcorn, "perhaps you should try the Aunt Sally; you'll be good at that!"

He was right, Jackie was extremely good at throwing balls at shelves of old crockery and enjoyed the sound of smashing as she hit the mark and scattered broken pottery everywhere.

"That was a pound well spent," she said, "I really enjoyed all that destruction!"

"Your Mum had better watch out when you next help with the washing up!" Tom laughed. "Come on, we'd better get back to our stalls and let the others have a wander round."

Chapter Three: Disaster!

It was growing dark and nearly time for everyone to take down their stands and tidy up. The Fair had been a great success and the children had really enjoyed running their stalls and looking around all the others. They had spent all their money and now were tired and ready to go home after the long day. Everyone, that is, apart from Laura. All day she had gone from stall to stall, collecting the money, writing in her notebook and carefully locking the cash in her box. But as the box got heavier and heavier, her mood got heavier and heavier too.

"It's just not fair, I've done all the hard work and nobody cares about me," she sulked. "Everybody's had a good day except me."

She forgot that Tom and then Sameer had offered to look after the cash box for her so she could wander around the stalls and buy some cakes and sweets. But she hadn't trusted anyone to look after it properly and now she was thoroughly fed up. She looked at everybody's happy and excited faces and made a decision.

"Ok, if they can have fun, so can I," she thought to herself. "I don't care! I'm going to throw the wet sponge at Mr Saunders and then I'm going to buy the chocolate cake that's been reduced on Amelia's stall."

She put the locked cash box in a supermarket bag and looking round saw she could hide it under Jill and Jackie's sweet stall where the cloth hung down and would hide the bag from view.

"Keep an eye on my bag," she whispered to Jill who was clearing up the last few unsold marzipan squares, "I'll be back in five minutes."

Jill was too busy to notice that Laura had left anything under her table. She put the remaining sweets in a box, put the price labels in the rubbish bin and then started to wipe the table cloth before taking it off and folding it up.

Meanwhile Laura had found that, much to Mr Saunders' relief, she was no good at throwing wet sponges. Her first sponge landed miles in front of him and the others flew over his shoulders or above his head.

"Never mind, Laura, better luck at the summer fair," Mr Saunders called through chattering teeth. "But it won't be me," he thought, "never again!"

A light drizzle had started and a chilly breeze was blowing bits of paper round the playground. Laura shivered and, hurrying back into the brightly lit hall, was relieved to see that the chocolate cake was still for sale. She bought it and then saw a small pink knitted rabbit on the knitted toy stall. It was the last toy left and was looking so sorry for itself that she bought it for her little sister. Almost everything had gone from the Tombola stall and the Year Six boys running it were glad when her ticket won her the last box of chocolates.

"Good, now at last we can pack up and go home," said one of the boys. "Let's hurry up and go before they ask us to sweep up or empty the rubbish bins."

Laura turned round and was amazed to see that almost all the tables had been put away and everything tidied up. Slightly alarmed she hurried over to where Jackie and Jill were putting on their coats ready to go home. Her supermarket bag was nowhere in sight.

"Oh, thanks so much for looking after the cash box, I'll take it now and hand it over to Mr Jones," Laura said.

"What?" said Jill, "What are you talking about?"

"The cash box with all the money in it," Laura said impatiently, "I left it with you whilst I looked round the stalls. It's in a supermarket bag and I left it under your table, for you to look after."

"I haven't a clue what you're talking about," Jackie shrugged. "I thought you were supposed to be in charge of the money, not us."

"But I told Jill I was leaving it with you. I wasn't away long, where have you put it?" shrieked Laura, her voice rising in panic.

"Look, we haven't put it anywhere," Jill said crossly. "It's you that's put it down somewhere and now you can't remember where. Don't blame us; we're not the ones going to be in big trouble!"

"But it must be somewhere here, help me find it," screamed Laura. Tears streamed down her face as the awful realisation dawned on her that the box with all the money in it had disappeared. Just then Tom and Sameer appeared. They'd had a great day and were chatting happily together but when they saw Laura's tear-streaked face they realised something terrible had happened.

"The money, it's gone!" sobbed Laura, "what am I going to do?"

"It must be here somewhere," Tom said calmly after he'd heard the sorry tale. "Come on there are five of us. Let's split up and search in all the corners and in the bins and everybody's bags."

Chapter Four: Panic!

In no time at all, five whirlwinds had hit the school hall. Bins were upturned, bags were opened and furniture was moved. But by now nearly everyone had gone home, the hall was almost empty and it soon became obvious that the cash box was not there. Laura couldn't believe that this was happening to her. Huge sobs wracked her body and she felt she could hardly breathe. She rushed out into the playground and took massive gulps of cold air. The rain had turned to sleet and was drifting down from a pitch black sky. It shone eerily white in the lamp light, making Laura feel that she was in the middle of some weird nightmare. Everything had been tidied away and everyone seemed to have gone home. Desperately, Laura ran back and forth, searching in the dark corners for any sign of the money box. She was soon soaking wet, her hair plastered to her head, her thin jumper clinging to her body.

"What am I going to do? What's going to happen to me?" she sobbed. "How am I going to tell Mr Jones; he's going to kill me!"

At that moment a huge orange shape seemed to appear from nowhere. It loomed over her and put its arms round her. Laura screamed in terror as the smell of rubber enveloped her and then a kind voice said,

"Whatever's the matter? Who's going to kill you?" It was Mr Saunders, still in his wetsuit and carrying a sponge and a bucket. Relief flooded through Laura and for a moment she leaned against the damp, rubbery teacher. By now she was shivering uncontrollably, from cold, fright and panic and seemed to have become speechless. Mr Saunders led her back into the hall where the others were now looking for Laura as well as the cash box.

"There you are!" shouted Sameer, "We thought we'd lost you as well as the money."

"Here, put your coat on," Jill said; "you look like a drowned rat."

"Yes, and you'd better sit down before you fall down," Tom said kindly. "You look awful."

Laura sank shakily onto a chair, put her face in her hands and burst into more tears.

"Well is someone going to tell me what all this is about?" Mr Saunders asked. "I can't imagine it can be that bad."

"It is, it is," muffled sobs came from Laura, "tell him what's happened, please."

So the others told Mr Saunders how Laura had been responsible for all the money collected by the class that day and how she had lost it. Mr Saunders' face grew grimmer and grimmer and even though he looked rather ridiculous in his dripping orange wetsuit and wellies, the children knew he was horrified by their story.

Eventually Laura spoke. In a quavering voice no more than a whisper she explained how she had looked after the money all day, had counted it carefully and hadn't let it out of her sight until she had left it for ten minutes, thinking that Jill was keeping an eye on it.

Then Mr Saunders asked the question no one had dared to ask Laura before:

"Laura, how much money was in the cash box?"

"Almost five hundred pounds," she whispered, "four hundred and eighty-five pounds and fifty pence, plus the three pounds I was going to put in for the things I bought."

There was a sharp intake of breath from everyone. None of them had imagined there would be so much money in the box, and now it was lost.

"Well, it's much worse than I imagined," Mr Saunders said quietly. "We all know you didn't mean to lose the money, Laura, but this is very serious. Not only have we lost almost five hundred pounds, we also have a thief around. We must go and see Mr Jones right away; he'll be in his office. Come on all of you."

The children were shocked. They had been so busy trying to find the money that they hadn't even thought about how it had disappeared.

"Of course," breathed Tom, "it's not lost, it's been stolen."

Laura couldn't decide if that made her feel better or worse. Perhaps it wasn't her fault, perhaps she hadn't been careless and it was the thief's fault. But she realised that two people had been at fault, her and the thief. If she hadn't left the money lying around then there would have been no chance for someone to steal it.

"Off you go, straight to The Head's office," Mr Saunders said, "I'll be right behind you; just give me five minutes to get out of this thing." He hurried off leaving the children staring miserably at each other.

"I'd better get it over and done with," Laura said bravely, "but you don't all have to come with me. It's me who's lost the money, not you."

"'Course we'll come with you; Mr Jones can be pretty scary when he's cross," Jill said, remembering the time she'd been in his office after she'd deliberately locked her sister in a cupboard during an argument and then lost the key.

"Well, I'll do the talking," Laura said shakily as they approached the Head's office and knocked on his door.

Chapter Five: Laura's Confession

"Come in," a cheery voice called. Mr Jones had enjoyed a good day and he was in a jolly mood. But as Laura miserably poured out her dreadful story, his smile disappeared, his brows furrowed and an angry dark red spread across his face.

"How could you have been so careless?" he spluttered angrily. "You knew there was a thief about and you promised you wouldn't let the money out of your sight for one second. I thought I could rely on you Laura; I'm very disappointed. And now not only have we lost all that money I'll have to get the police involved." Before anyone could say anything he'd picked up the phone. "Put me through to the police please, Miss Smith," he said to his secretary. Then looking at the children he said, "You may as well go home now, we'll sort this out on Monday, off you go; I have to deal with the police now."

"Oh please, Mr Jones, I'm so sorry; please forgive me, I'm so sorry," sobbed Laura but Mr Jones was already talking to the police and waved her impatiently away. Stunned, the children stood in the corridor outside the Head's door staring at each other.

"Well, that was awful," Tom said. "I've never seen him so cross."

"He didn't even give us a chance to explain properly," Jackie said indignantly; "he's so mean!"

"No, he's right," Laura said quietly, "It is my fault; I shouldn't have left the cash box lying around. He put his trust in me and I've let everyone down. It's just too dreadful."

At that moment Mr Saunders appeared, dressed in a navy blue track suit and looking quite normal again.

"Sorry kids, it took me ages to get out of that stupid wetsuit, how did you get on with Mr Jones?"

"He's so angry with Laura," Sameer said. "I don't think he'll ever forgive her."

"Well, there's nothing you can do now," advised Mr Saunders. "Just go home and let the police do their job. You never know, the money might have turned up by Monday morning. Let's just wait and see. I'll pop in to Mr Jones and put in a good word for you, Laura," he said kindly. "Try not to worry too much. Off you go."

The children walked home together slowly. Their mood was as dark as the night. Sleet swirled round them and everything was dreary and miserable. How different from this morning when they'd hurried cheerfully to school looking forward to a great day. And now everything was spoilt. It seemed to Laura that all she had to look forward to was a telling off from her parents and then an even worse telling off from Mr Jones on Monday morning. What would her punishment be she wondered? She couldn't pay the money back. Perhaps she'd have to stay in every break and dinner time and wash paint brushes and sharpen pencils? Or perhaps she wouldn't ever be allowed on any school trips ever again? The horrible possibilities were endless.

Before the children separated to go to their different homes they saw a police car speeding down the road towards school. Two grim looking officers were peering through the sleet and darkness as they went to investigate the theft of five hundred pounds and Laura's cash box.

Chapter Six: Forgiven!

Laura had spent a horrible weekend at home. Her parents were as shocked as she was and hadn't really told her off. They planned to go into school on Monday to plead her case.

"We'll go in and get all this sorted out," her dad had said. "I'm sure it's not all your fault."

"Yes Dad, it is my fault and I'm going to have to pay for it," Laura had said, dreading what Mr Jones was going to say to her. And now here she was at nine o'clock on Monday morning, standing outside the Head's office, her stomach doing somersaults and her knees shaking.

"Come in," Mr Jones called and Laura slid into the room, hardly daring to look at him. As soon as she saw Mr Jones' face she knew that her worst fears would be realised.

"Well, what have you got to say for yourself?" asked the Head sternly. "I have no idea why I thought I could trust you to collect all that money and look after it properly. And now you have lost a small fortune by leaving it lying around carelessly when you promised me you wouldn't let it out of your sight. That money is desperately needed by Heather House and now it's gone. I'm afraid I have no choice but to punish you severely Laura."

"Oh no," moaned Laura, "I'm so sorry I lost the money, Mr Jones."

"It's a bit late to be sorry now," Mr Jones snapped. "You should've thought of that before you left it lying around and went off to enjoy yourself. You will spend every break and lunch time picking up litter and tidying up the sports cupboards until the end of term. And of course you will not be going to the Bonfire Night Party this year. I hope that will teach you a lesson!"

Laura was totally dismayed. Working at break and dinner times was one thing but to miss the Bonfire Party was just too much. She had so been looking forward to selling her homemade parkin and joining in the excitement of the fireworks. She burst into loud sobs, tears streaming down her face and her nose running.

"Stop that noise," Mr Jones said crossly. "This punishment is only what you deserve!"

This only made Laura bawl louder and more fiercely until her nose was bright red and her face was all splotchy. After a while she couldn't cry anymore and her sobs turned into hiccups and gradually died away. Wiping her nose on her sleeve because she couldn't find a tissue, she looked up at Mr Jones and spoke in a low shaky voice.

"I'm so sorry Mr Jones. I know I was silly and selfish to leave the money under the table. I'll never be able to repay it, but please forgive me, please." Her quiet voice faded away and she started to cry silently, huge tears coursing down her bright red cheeks. Her shoulders shook and she hung her head in shame and misery, not daring to look at Mr Jones' angry face. After what seemed like a lifetime she heard him speaking softly.

"Ok Laura, stop crying. I can see how sorry you are. I have changed my mind and have decided not to punish you. Now take a tissue from the box, tidy yourself up and go back to your classroom. I'll see you at the Bonfire Party."

At first Laura could hardly believe her ears. She looked up and stared at Mr Jones in amazement. A kind smile had spread across his face and his eyes were twinkling.

"Oh thank you, thank you!" gasped Laura. "I can't believe it! Oh thank you!"

"Come on, off you go, I haven't got all day," he said gently. "Tell your friends you're forgiven and it's all forgotten. We'll let the police do their job and find the thief."

Laura felt as though she was floating down the corridor as she returned to the classroom. This really was unbelievable, totally forgiven; totally free! Amelia looked up as Laura opened the door and was astonished to see her smiling.

"What happened?" Amelia whispered.

"He's let me off, it's alright!" grinned Laura, "I'll tell you at break," she added as the teacher asked everyone to get ready for their Monday morning tables test:

"Hurry up Laura, we've wasted enough time waiting for you already," she remarked. "You can talk to your friends at the proper time."

The Fern Valley Venturers gathered round Laura at break, thrilled and excited as she told them she was forgiven and wasn't going to be punished for her silly mistake.

"I can hardly believe he said you can forget all about it," said Ali.

"It's fantastic, now we can look forward to The Grand Bonfire Party. It's going to be so much fun, and we can raise more money for Heather House as well," Sameer said.

"As long as I'm not looking after it," Laura laughed happily.

Chapter Seven: Parkin and all things Treacle

With the awful circumstances of the Fair behind them, the children could indeed plan for their part in the School Bonfire Night celebrations. With others from their class the girls had been asked to be in charge of the stall selling toffee apples, treacle toffee and parkin. Jill and Jackie were going to make some of the treacle toffee and toffee apples and Laura and Amelia were helping to prepare the parkin.

"Whatever is all this strange food we're going to eat? I've never even heard of it," Sameer had asked. He hadn't been living in England for very long and although he'd learnt all about Guy Fawkes and the Gunpowder Plot in History, he'd certainly never come across treacle and parkin in his own country.

"It's just traditional food," said Tom. "I think treacle toffee was first made here hundreds of years ago."

"It's sometimes called Plot Toffee, you know, after the Gunpowder Plot," Laura said importantly, "but toffee apples were invented in America only about two hundred years ago, so it's not very traditional."

"Ok clever clogs, so if you know that, tell us what parkin is," Jill asked.

"It's a sort of gingerbread cake made with syrup and brown sugar, all soft and squishy," interrupted Amelia, "Laura's not the only one who reads books you know."

"Sounds yummy," Sameer said, ignoring Laura and Amelia who were glaring at each other, "I can't wait to try it."

"Well, us boys have got the most important job of all," Ali said.

"Oh yes, collecting wood and building the bonfire on the field," Tom said. "You can't have Bonfire Night without a bonfire. We've already collected loads of twigs and branches and the Year Six boys are going to help us make the bonfire."

"Well, we've only got a few days before the Bonfire on Saturday so we're going to be pretty busy each day after school," remarked Jill.

"But what about Halloween tonight, I thought we were going to go Trick and Treating?" Jackie said. "We've got those scary masks to wear."

"Mum and Dad won't let me go Trick and Treating," Amelia said, "and I don't like those horrible costumes with blood and stuff all over."

"Don't be so babyish," Jackie snorted, "it's only a bit of fun."

"No, Laura's right," Sameer said suddenly. "It's not really fun at all. Why would you want to play being dead or want to be a skeleton or pretend to be injured and covered in blood? I've seen what it's really like, and it's not funny."

They all stared at Sameer and remembered why he and his family had come to live in England last year. The silence was finally broken by the bell for the end of play and as they trooped back into school the others overheard Jill talking to Jackie:

214

"Ok then, no Trick or Treating and scary masks. We can make some more treacle toffee instead." Jackie nodded her head in agreement and Sameer smiled sadly to himself.

Chapter Eight: A Nasty Incident

By Thursday the children could hardly contain their excitement. There were only two more days to go before Bonfire Night. The pile of wood and branches at the far end of the field was huge and that evening the boys were going to build it into the biggest bonfire they'd ever seen. There was going to be a low fence all around to keep people from getting too near and the adults had chosen the firework area well away from shooting sparks and drifting embers.

"They're going to set off the fireworks over here," Ali said, pointing to a flat open area away from trees and buildings. "My Dad is in charge of organising the display. They've spent a fortune on buying the fireworks and have worked out the show, it's going to last about twenty minutes and it's going to be great."

"I hope they have lots of rockets," Jill said excitedly. "I love it when they whoosh up into the sky and then burst into all those different colours."

"Yes, and lots of bangs and screams, the louder the better for me," added Jackie."

"I prefer the quieter ones like the snow-fountains and Roman candles," Amelia said.

"Even Roman candles finish with a bang; I like the giant Catherine Wheels best," Laura said. She was still amazed that she was allowed to join in all the fun. Every time she thought of her disaster her stomach lurched with horror and then she remembered she was forgiven and breathed a sigh of relief.

"I wonder if The Fern Valley Venturers will have an adventure on Bonfire Night?" remarked Jim. "After all, there is a thief about and I think we should be on the lookout for anything suspicious going on."

"Well you were the one who found the boy who was stealing when we were on the dig," said Sameer, "so perhaps you can track down the person who stole the cash box as well."

"Yes, we should organise lookouts and decide how to keep in touch with each other in case we see someone acting suspiciously," Ali said excitedly. "I bet the thief will be back to try again."

As they were pondering how to catch the thief, Laura suddenly jumped up and yelled, "Hey, you, come here!" They saw her pointing and waving to a small startled girl.

"That's Kelly from Year Four, she owes me five pounds from the Fair," she said sharply. "She didn't give me the last of the money from her DVD stall. I'm going to ask her for it."

"Well she won't be walking round with it at school," Tom said doubtfully, rather surprised at Laura's fierce tone of voice.

"Hey Kelly," Laura shouted, "have you got that five pounds you owe me? I want it now!"

Startled, Kelly stopped in her tracks and stammered,

"Oh hello Laura, no, I was going to tell you. Instead of giving it to you to put in your cash box, I bought some perfume for my Mum from The Cosmetics stall and so that money and the money I owed you went into their collection for Heather House instead of yours. I hope that's alright?"

"What?" screamed Laura, "You should've put it in my cash box, that's my money and I want it back."

"But you lost all the money in your cash box, Laura," Amelia reminded her.

"Shut up Amelia. It's none of your business," shrieked Laura. "It's my money and I want it back now!"

Her face had turned dark red with anger and she went up to Kelly and shook her by the shoulders.

"NOW!" she repeated fiercely.

Kelly burst into tears,

"I'm sorry Laura, I haven't got it. I'm sorry, I should've put it in your cash box but I didn't and now I haven't got it to give to you."

"You owe me five pounds," Laura repeated in a dark menacing voice, "and I want it now."

"But she's just said she hasn't got it," protested Sameer. "How can she give it you if she hasn't got it?"

"She'll have to pay me from her own pocket money," Laura snapped.

"But I only get fifty pence a week," Kelly wailed.

"Well you'll have to give me fifty pence for the next ten weeks won't you?" Laura replied. "And make sure you don't miss a week, I want it as soon as possible."

"But I was saving up to buy Christmas presents for Mum and Dad," sobbed Kelly, who by now was looking terrified.

"Well tough, they won't be getting any presents this year will they?" Laura said triumphantly. "Remember, fifty pence every week, and I won't let you forget," she said menacingly, giving Kelly a hard push.

Kelly walked shakily away and the Fern Valley Venturers stared at Laura in silent horror. Jim eventually broke the silence.

"That was really mean of you Laura," he protested, "Kelly doesn't really owe you five pounds, she just put it in someone else's cash box and it will go to Heather House all the same."

"Yes," Ali chipped in, "look how much money you lost and Mr Jones let you off all of it, and now you won't forgive Kelly just five pounds."

"Well I don't care," Laura said harshly, "I want my money and I'm going to get it!"

With that she turned sharply and walked away leaving her friends staring at her back, shocked and upset.

"I just don't know what's got into her," Amelia remarked miserably, "she's turned horrible."

"Yes, she was so unfair to Kelly," Jill agreed.

"Well there's only one thing for it," Jackie announced dramatically.

"What?" they all chorused.

"Well of course we'll have to tell Mr Jones what Laura has done," Jackie answered.

"Do you really think we should?" Amelia asked, "She might get into terrible trouble."

"Serve her right if she does," Jackie replied. "Come on, who's coming with me to see the Head?" At first there was silence and no one moved until gradually, one by one they each nodded in agreement and started to follow Jackie towards Mr Jones' office. The Fern Valley Venturers had had their occasional disagreements in the past, but this was something different. Laura's terrible behaviour had shocked them so much they knew they would have to do something about it, even if it meant hurting one of them. Then to their surprise they heard a voice behind them,

"Hey you lot, where are you going? Wait for me, I'm coming too."

It was Laura who seemed to have forgotten her bad-tempered outburst and was running up behind them with a big smile on her face. But when she saw all her friends silently staring at her, her smile faded and her steps faltered.

"Oh Laura, we're going to tell Mr Jones what you've done," Amelia said, "I don't think you should come with us."

"Of course I should, why not?" asked Laura, "I haven't done anything wrong."

Chapter Nine: The Verdict

And so it was that all eight Fern Valley Venturers crammed into the Head's office as Mr Jones listened in astonishment to how Laura had treated Kelly from Year Four.

"Is this true Laura?" he asked, "Did you really do that to Kelly? After I forgave you for losing five hundred pounds are you really trying to get Kelly to give you the five pounds you think she owes you?" Before Laura could answer he continued,

"Don't you see that if I was kind enough to forgive you five hundred pounds, you should have been just as kind and forgiven Kelly the little bit she owes you? I'm sorry, this is really serious. My verdict is this: you will stay in at break and lunchtime to pick up litter, tidy the PE cupboards, sharpen the pencils and wash the paint brushes in all the classrooms up until Easter. And of course you certainly won't be going to the Bonfire Party. Someone else will help Amelia sell the parkin you made while you will stay at home and miss all the fun. I hope this will make you understand how badly you have behaved."

A terrible hush fell over the children as they listened to Mr Jones' shocking verdict. Only Laura didn't agree with the Head's punishment and without another word she rushed out of the room, slamming the door behind her.

"Well children," Mr Jones said sadly, "I am sorry about Laura's harsh punishment but I really think it is what she deserves. If you are forgiven a lot then you should be able to forgive a little."

The children nodded in agreement and shuffled miserably out of the office. It was the end of lunch break and time to go back to their classroom.

"We'll meet after school," Tom hissed to the others, "and decide what to do next."

Most of the afternoon was spent painting Bonfire pictures. It should have been fun but the Fern Valley Venturers didn't really have the heart for it, especially Laura when she was told she had to wash all the paint pots, brushes and palettes after the lesson.

Finally it was time to go home and the friends met together in the playground, apart from Laura who had stormed off home after she had tidied up the paints.

"Oh dear," Amelia said, "Laura blames us for getting her into trouble; I don't think she'll ever speak to me again. What are we going to do?"

"What we're going to do is not let her spoil all our fun," replied Jackie firmly. "It's her own fault and she'll just have to put up with it."

"I agree," Jim said, "come on everyone, cheer up, we've got a bonfire to build tonight! Us boys are going to help the Year Sixes so we've got to go home and get changed into our scruffiest clothes and come back before it gets too dark. Come on hurry up!"

With that the four boys raced off home together.

"He's right," Jill said, "we've got stuff to do too. We've still got more treacle toffee to make and the toffee apples to wrap. Come round to our house to help us, Amelia, and we'll help you wrap the parkin you've made."

And so it was that the Fern Valley Venturers put the unpleasant Laura incident behind them and set out to enjoy the best Bonfire Night ever. Little did they know exactly how exciting it was going to turn out to be!

Chapter Ten: Treasure

By late Saturday afternoon everything was prepared. All the stalls selling food and drink were set up and loaded with goodies. Jill and Jackie's treacle stall looked very inviting and with help from two other friends, Amelia had filled her stall with delicious looking parkin. There were some sideshows, a platform for the brass band, a stall where you could buy sparklers and a tent for a baby and toddler crèche. All sorts of tables and platforms covered the firework display area which had been cordoned off with red tape and there were several fire extinguishers and buckets of water and sand nearby in case of emergencies. All that was needed was for the fireworks themselves to be brought out in their big tin boxes just before the display was to start. But the best bit of all was the huge bonfire the boys had built on the other side of the field. It towered up into the sky in a pyramid shape and they couldn't wait to see the magnificent blaze it would make. It was Tom and Ali's job to carefully crawl round the fire before it was lit to make sure there were no hedgehogs curled up in the shelter of the branches and twigs. The fire was due to be set ablaze at six o'clock and so at five, torches in their hands, they approached the massive mountain of wood. They crept under the little surrounding fence and crawling carefully around, shining the torches and using long sticks to prod the wood, they checked for hibernating animals or small sleeping children.

"After all, this would make a great den to hide in if you were little," chuckled Ali.

Just as their check was almost complete Tom's torch shone on something shiny buried deep inside the bonfire.

"Stop, wait, what's that?" he said excitedly.

"Gosh," Ali replied, "I don't know. Hang on a minute, I'll use this stick to try and reach it." Using a long stick and stretching as far as he could, he just managed to touch the object. It made a sort of metallic sound as he prodded it.

"Well that's not wood and I'm sure it shouldn't be in the bonfire," Tom said. "Let's try to hook it out."

Down on their hands and knees, with a long stick each they prodded and poked the object towards them until Tom could stretch out and grab it with his fingertips.

"I don't believe it!" he gasped as he dragged the find through the twigs. "Look what it is!"

Panting with the effort and lying flat on their tummies in the grass they both stared in astonishment at the black, rectangular, metal box in front of them.

"It's a cash box," whispered Ali. "Do you think it's the one Laura lost?"

"Well let's open it and see," said Tom. "Look the key is attached to it by string like Laura's was."

Whilst Ali shone the torch, Tom fiddled with the lock until it opened with a click and he threw back the lid. There, revealed in the beam of the torch nestled a pile of five and ten pound notes.

"It must be Laura's stolen box. The thief has hidden it in the bonfire, but whatever for?" wondered Ali.

"Quick, let's put it back," Tom said urgently. "The thief has obviously hidden it here where he thought nobody would find it. But he'll be back to get it soon before the bonfire's lit. And we'll be here to get him!"

Hurriedly they closed and locked the box and were just about to shove it back into the middle of the bonfire when Ali had an idea.

"No, let's keep it. When the thief comes back and can't find it he'll get into a panic and think he's looking in the wrong place. That will give us more time to get help and catch him."

"Good idea," agreed Tom," and at least there'll be no danger of him escaping and running off with the money."

He stuffed the box inside his coat and stood up. He found that if he kept his arm to his side the box stayed firmly in place.

"No one will notice it, "laughed Ali. "You've got so many jumpers on under your coat you already look twice your usual size!"

It was true. The weather was bitterly cold and they were both wearing extra jumpers as well as hats, scarves and gloves.

"Speak for yourself," grinned Tom, "you look like Boy Mountain. But come on, let's go and tell the others we're on the lookout for The Cash Box Thief, we'll need all the help we can get."

"Where've you been?" Jim asked as they hurried to meet him and Sameer by the hot dog stall. "The Baby fireworks are starting soon and I want to get a good place to see them from."

Before the bonfire was lit and the main firework display started, there was going to be a short display of quiet, pretty fireworks for the younger children.

"I didn't know you were a baby," started Sameer but he was interrupted by Tom.

"Never mind the Baby fireworks," he gasped, "we've some news for you. We've found Laura's cash box with all the money in it hidden in the middle of the bonfire. We reckon the thief will be back soon to get it before the bonfire is lit."

"Well what are we waiting for?" asked an astonished Sameer, "that means he'll be back any minute now. What's our plan?"

"There are four of us. I reckon we should spread out round the edge of the bonfire and whoever sees him first should give a shout," suggested Tom. "Then we can all run round and pounce on him."

"Don't you think we should tell some of the grownups?" Ali said doubtfully. "We don't want him to get away."

"We haven't got time for that," objected Tom; "it'll take too long to explain and they probably wouldn't believe us anyway. The

228

important thing is to get back to the bonfire. Hurry up, the Baby fireworks are starting. I bet he'll come when everyone is watching them."

Chapter Eleven: A False Accusation

The four boys hurried back to the bonfire and spread themselves out around its edge just outside the low fence. It loomed up like a dark mountain against the black sky and in the gloomy shadows it really was very difficult to see anything at all. Just then a shower of Silver Storms and Catherine Wheels threw their white and yellow lights up into the sky and there were oohs and aahs from the young children watching. The bonfire, the field and all the people were lit up in the bright glare and then disappeared from sight as the fireworks died down.

Sameer shivered slightly at the sounds and then reminded himself that these were just fireworks and he was safe in England.

"I don't know how we're even going to see the thief, never mind catch him," thought Ali gloomily. "I'm sure we should've told some of the adults."

Next Roman Candles sent up balls of red, blue, yellow and green lights and some Violet Volcanoes cast an eerie purple light over the field. At that moment Sameer saw a dark shape loom up from the shadows, silhouetted against the light of the fireworks.

"Over there!" he yelled, "near you, Tom."

The fireworks faded and everything was plunged into darkness again but not before Tom caught a glimpse of a man creeping towards him. Tom let out a blood curdling scream and threw himself at the man, knocking him to the ground. The man tried to crawl away but

Tom grabbed him by his legs and hung on. As he fell, the cash box hidden under his coat crashed onto the ground and the lid flew open scattering notes everywhere. By now the other boys were there to help. Ali gathered up as much money as he could and stuffed it into his pockets while Sameer and Jim tried to help Tom with the man. But he was large and very strong. He kicked and wriggled, lashing out with his feet and arms and the boys could not get a grip on him. In one last effort the man struggled free from the boys, grabbed the cash box and ran off.

"Stop Thief!" yelled the boys, "Help! Help!" But it was too late, the man had escaped.

Hearing their shouts, Mr Saunders and a few parents soon arrived on the scene where a bright white light from a dozen Silver Showers was making it as bright as day. They found four boys lying on the ground in a heap on top of each other.

"Whatever's going on?" Mr Saunders asked. "Did you say you'd caught the thief?" Slowly the boys got to their feet and brushed themselves down. A five pound note fluttered onto the ground from Ali's coat and Mr Saunders pounced on him.

"Well, I never would have thought it," he gasped. "You, a thief? Come on then, empty your pockets; let's see what you've got."

"But Mr Saunders…….." the boys chorused, "it's not……….."

"Be quiet boys, this is a very serious matter," snapped Mr Saunders as he watched Ali pull out fistfuls of money from his various coat pockets.

"There must be hundreds of pounds here," Mr Saunders said grimly. "I can't tell you how disappointed I am in you Ali. You'd better come with me and I'll take you to Mr Jones after the firework display. He'll be too busy to deal with you now. Well done boys," he said turning to the others, "you've done a better job than the police!"

"But Mr Saunders, you've got it all wrong," Tom stammered. "We haven't caught the thief, it's not Ali."

"Well, I'm afraid it's no use trying to defend your friend, Tom. We've caught Ali red-handed and there's no more to be said. I'm sure the Head will want to see you later, and the police may want to interview you too. Now just enjoy the firework display, it will be starting soon. Come with me Ali, I'm not letting you out of my sight."

With that he marched off, a heavy hand on Ali's shoulder. Ali turned round to look helplessly at his friends. Tears were streaming down his face and even as he walked away a ten pound note fell out of a pocket and floated to the ground.

"Don't worry, Ali," Tom called, "we'll sort it out."

"And just how are we going to do that?" Sameer asked angrily. "Ali was right; we should've got some grownups to help us. And now look what trouble he's in."

"Yes, who's going to believe us?" Jim asked. "He really does look very guilty. How are we going to prove he's not the thief?"

"By catching the real one of course," Tom said triumphantly. "I bet you anything he'll come back for the money when he finds the cash box is almost empty and then we'll be ready for him."

A blue light filled the air as dozens of Sky Rays showered sparks and balls of fire into the sky for the finale of the Baby firework display. The light revealed three young boys staring intently at each other. Sameer and Jim looked miserable and angry but Tom's eyes shone with hope and excitement.

"There's still some time before the bonfire's lit," Tom said. "Let's go and tell the girls what's happened and see if they've got any ideas. And, I'm starving; I could murder a hot dog!"

"How can you think about food at a time like this when Ali's been hauled off by Mr Saunders and we still haven't caught the real thief?" Jim asked. "I just feel like going home."

"Don't be like that," Sameer said, "perhaps Tom's right after all and we can catch the thief and prove Ali is innocent. Besides, I want to give this parking a try; let's go and see the girls."

"It's parkin, silly," Jim smiled. "Alright let's go and see what the girls have to say, but we'll have to hurry up."

The girls had a lot to say! As the boys tucked into hot dogs and parkin Jill said how pathetic the boys had been to let the man get away and Jackie said she couldn't believe they'd let Mr Saunders think Ali was the thief.

"One thing's for sure," Amelia said, "we're coming with you this time. You obviously can't be trusted to get things right without us!"

Tom would have objected but his teeth were stuck together with treacle toffee and besides he knew that they needed the girl's help if they were going to be successful.

"Ok," he said finally, wiping his sticky mouth on his sleeve, "who's got any suggestions?"

"Well," Jackie said, "I reckon he'll wait until the main firework display has started then he'll come back and sneak around the bonfire looking for the money when everyone is watching the fireworks."

"Yes, he will have realised the money fell out of the cash box when we were wrestling with him and will be hoping it's still there by the fire," Jill added.

"But he won't be able to get near the bonfire when it's lit, there's the fence all around it and stewards there to stop people getting too close, and it will be really hot," Amelia said.

"Well if he wants to get the money back that's the risk he'll have to take," Jim said, "and this time there'll be plenty of people around to help us catch him."

"It's five minutes to lighting the bonfire. Let's get into our positions before it's lit," Tom said. "And remember that when the firework display is going on, we've got to keep a look out for the thief and not watch the fireworks."

"We can leave the stalls now," Jill said. "We've almost sold out and everyone is moving over to the fire; come on before we're stuck at the back."

Chapter Twelve: To Catch a Thief

The crowd was walking over to the bonfire, chattering excitedly. Many fastened their coats tightly round themselves and pulled their hats over their ears shivering in the cold night. A strong breeze had sprung up and flags, tablecloths and tents could be heard flapping in the wind. Just inside the low fence, several of the parents in luminous jackets walked round the fire doing a last check, shining their torches here and there to make sure all was clear. Then one by one they each took a long stemmed lighter called a port fire and set light to small clumps of twigs scattered round the base of the fire. At first nothing seemed to happen and then to murmurs of excitement the kindling caught fire and started to burn. It was amazing how quickly the flames spread and started to leap upwards, igniting the bigger branches above. Soon with the wind fanning the flames the whole bonfire was ablaze and there was a roar and a whoosh and the sound of crackling. The smell of burning wood and smoke wafted over the crowd which made some people cough. As the blaze took hold it soon became too hot to stand near and the children realised they would have to stand quite a distance from the fire if they weren't going to be roasted alive. As people were warmed by the fire and then started to feel uncomfortably hot, they started to move away from it towards the firework display area. Soon only the six Fern Valley Venturers and the stewards remained near the fire. Some of the stewards stood with their backs to the blaze to make sure no one got too close, and some stood facing the flames watching that the fire didn't topple over or start to burn dangerously.

"Hey you kids, what are you still doing here?" one of the men called to Sameer. "The firework show is starting soon and you won't get a very good view from here."

"Erm, we're just waiting for someone," Sameer mumbled. He wished they'd decided before if they were going to tell the stewards about their plan to catch a thief. In fact he realised they didn't really have a plan at all. Jim was realising the same thing as he too made up some excuse for hanging around the bonfire when everyone else was at the display site. Even Tom wondered exactly what they were going to do if and when the thief reappeared. He was just going to tell the steward nearest him that that they were planning to catch a thief who had stolen a money box when he realised how silly it sounded. And then the firework display started with several huge shrieks and explosions as rockets shot up into the sky showering great balls of coloured fire into space. From a distance Tom could see the men, including Ali's dad, in the display area moving about in the dark, their lighters glowing as they went to a nearby platform to light the next set of fireworks. This time, great balls of coloured flame leapt up into the air and popped and exploded above their heads. Soon the men were moving to another platform and taking fireworks out of the tin boxes, they set them up carefully on the table and standing well back lit them. Great sheets of white light shot up into the air and then turned into yellow stars which popped and banged all around them. People shouted and clapped and cheered, thoroughly entranced by the show. Tom was enjoying the display so much he almost forgot he was meant to be looking out for a man creeping about in the shadows. He quickly turned his head back to the fire and saw all the stewards and all the Fern Valley Venturers staring up at the magnificent display of fire art.

"This is ridiculous," he thought, "the thief could come and steal the whole bonfire without any of us even noticing!" He turned his back on the display and stared into the shadows round the edge of the bonfire. He couldn't see much after staring at the bright lights of the fireworks and it took his eyes quite a long time to adjust to the dark. He decided to walk slowly round the bonfire and further out into the field in the direction the man had run off in before. The further away he went from the fire, the darker and colder it got and the more frightened he became. What on earth was he doing, a young boy trying to catch a criminal by himself? How stupid he had been to think he could tackle a man at least twice his size who was desperately looking for money he had lost. Perhaps he would return with a knife or even a gun? He was so caught up in his thoughts that indeed Tom did not notice the shadowy figure to his left creeping towards him. Before he realised it, a man's hand was over his mouth and a fierce voice was whispering in his ear.

"One squeak from you and you're a goner. Lie still while I tie you up."

The man's hot, horrible smelling breath wafted over his face and then Tom felt tape being stuck over his mouth and something being tied round his ankles. The man gave him a kick in the ribs and then crept away leaving Tom alone in the dark, a terrified, helpless bundle.

"Where's Tom gone?" wondered Jim a few minutes later, "he's completely disappeared." After realising that he'd been watching the fireworks and not looking out for the thief, Jim looked round for his friends. He could see the three girls standing round one side of the bonfire and Sameer at the other side, but no sign of Tom.

Chapter Thirteen: Fireworks!

As Jim wondered if he should go and look for Tom or stay where he was, a huge wall of orange flame leapt up into the sky from the display area and a series of pops and bangs pierced the air. There were screams from the crowd as yet another sheet of orange light lit up the sky. The stewards round the fire rushed towards the fireworks and Jim realised something must have gone wrong with the display which had become dangerously out of control. As another sheet of flame filled the air Jim saw silhouetted against the light a large dark shape crawling around the edge of the bonfire nearby. With a jolt Jim realised it was their thief back again. Indeed as Jim watched, the man grabbed something from the ground and put it into his pocket

"That must be some of the money Ali didn't pick up," thought Jim in a panic. "What am I going to do now? The others are too far away to see him, the stewards have gone and nobody will hear me shouting above the sound of the fireworks. I guess it's up to me."

Without another thought Jim took a running jump and landed on top of the man with a thump. Surprised, the man grunted in pain and rolled over onto his side taking Jim with him. Jim hung onto the man's coat, determined not to let him escape a second time. It was only when he felt a burning along his back that he realised the two of them had rolled as one body under the fence and were dangerously near the bonfire itself. Jim could smell his singeing clothes and realised his danger. The man realised too because he leapt up, shook himself free of Jim's grip and stumbled off in the direction of the fireworks. For a moment Jim lay dangerously near the bonfire, but the dreadful heat and the awful thought that the man was going to escape again made him leap up and race after him. A sheet of orange flame burned before him and in its light Jim saw the man run straight into the display area. He realised that no one else was left there because they had all fled the dangerous fiery inferno. Jim stopped in his tracks and raised his arm to shield his face from the searing light and heat. To his amazement he saw the dark shape of the man running towards the tins of fireworks which still hadn't been set off. He grabbed several of the large tins and started back towards the bonfire. Jim was relieved to see that the stewards had now reappeared and were pouring buckets of water and sand over the orange flames in front of him. They soon died down and there was a cheer from the spectators who were standing a safe distance away.

"Thank goodness," thought Jim, "but where are the others and whatever is the man going to do with all those tins of fireworks?"

He didn't have to wait long to find out. Running past Jim and within a few metres of him, the man was heading straight for the bonfire. Stopping at the edge he opened the tins and one by one threw them onto the bonfire and stepped back quickly.

"Run away, get down!" screamed Jim at the top of his voice as he saw his friends approaching. "The bonfire's going to explode, run away."

No sooner had he screamed his warning than the bonfire did indeed explode. Rockets whizzed out at all angles, screaming away at head height and then bursting into showers of multi-coloured stars as they hit the ground. Roman candles shot out their colours of red, blue and green with loud pops and bangs. Firebombs leapt out of the bonfire with almighty explosions and rip-raps cracked and hissed from the middle of the bonfire.

Jim lay flat on his stomach, his arms over his head and prayed that it would come to an end. He didn't have time to wonder if his friends were safe, and thoughts of the man who had caused all this chaos didn't enter his head. It was taking him all his effort just to survive. After what seemed like an age of loud noises and searing lights, Jim heard men shouting and the hiss of water on fire. He carefully raised his head and looked round. Everything had gone dark and Jim realised that the bonfire had been put out. Men were walking round with torches, bending over nearby huddles on the ground and with a gulp Jim realised they were his friends who had been the only ones near the bonfire when it exploded. Getting up on his hands and knees he crawled to the nearest huddle. It was Jackie and Jill, their arms tightly clasped round each other.

"We're alright, "Jackie said in a trembling voice, "but you'd better check on Sameer."

"Yes, remember that he's terrified of fireworks," Jill whispered. "This was bad enough for us; imagine what it was like for him. He must have felt he was back in the middle of the war in his country."

Shocked at the thought of Sameer's terror, Jim hurried to the next bundle on the ground. It was shaking and sobbing and one of the stewards was already lifting Sameer up and offering him a drink.

"Don't worry, lad, you're safe now," the kind man said. "Take your time and then we'll take you to somewhere warm and more comfortable."

Jim threw himself down next to Sameer but before he could speak Sameer said shakily, "Well if that's what your English Bonfire Nights are like, I won't be going to another. It was just like the night men came to our village with guns, and planes flew overhead and dropped bombs on us." He gave a sob and a hiccup and wiped the tears from his face and then he smiled, "And I don't even like that parking much!" Jim was so relieved to see that Sameer was alright.

"I'm so sorry, Sameer, it all went wrong. I really don't know what happened."

"Well," the steward said, "I do. One of the firework men accidently dropped his lighter into two big boxes of Orange Sunbursts and they all went off together. Incredibly nobody was hurt and everyone got away in time but it took us a while to put the flames out. I suppose it was really a good job it happened because everyone had already moved away by the time that maniac ran into the display area and grabbed the tins of fireworks and threw them onto the bonfire. You kids were the only ones around and it's a miracle none of you was hurt. Just the little girl was hit by part of a Roman candle which burned her coat, but she's alright."

"Amelia!" said Jim, "I must find her."

"They've taken her to the first aid tent," the steward continued, "and that's where I'm taking you two to be checked out, you look awful. Someone's already taken the twins. At least they've caught that mad man. He ran straight into the arms of Mr Saunders and he tackled him to the ground. That Mr Saunders is quite a hero. Apparently the man was the one who took the cash box at the Autumn Fair. They say he was here to get it back and to steal more from the stalls tonight. Mr Saunders caught him trying to run off with the money from the parkin and treacle toffee stalls. I reckon the police will be here by now to cart him off. Serve him right, he could have got someone seriously injured tonight. Well, all's well that ends well."

Whether it was delayed shock or relief that the man had been caught Jim didn't know, but all of a sudden he found himself crying big gulping sobs and giant tears rushed down his cheeks making tracks in his dusty face.

"Come on, you two, let's get you checked out, you've been through a lot tonight," said the steward.

"Little do you know," Jim thought as he and Sameer made their way slowly to the first-aid tent, arm in arm, both supporting each other. "This has been the worst of our adventures and not much fun at all."

Chapter Fourteen: A Rescue and a Resolution

The Bonfire Party had finished and most people were going home. It hadn't been a very successful night what with the boxes of flaming Orange Sunbursts exploding and then the bonfire shooting rockets and fireworks everywhere, not to mention the presence of a mad thief. Jim wondered if they would have another Bonfire next year and somehow doubted it. He just hoped they'd raised enough money to give to Heather House.

Sitting in the tent Jackie, Jill and Amelia were wrapped in bright red blankets sipping mugs of hot chocolate and chatting happily together.

"Thank goodness you're alright!" Jim burst out.

"Gosh, you two look terrible," Jill said looking Sameer and Jim up and down. Peering at Sameer's dusty, tear stained face and his filthy clothes, Jim realised he must look just as bad.

"And what's happened to the back of your coat?" Jackie asked, "it's all orange and brown and you smell awful."

Jim bent round and saw to his horror that the back of his coat was singed brown and in some places was burnt black. He realised how close he had been to going up in flames as he had lain near the bonfire. Amelia's coat had similar marks where the Roman candle had hit it. It seemed they had both had narrow escapes.

"Well, at least we're all safe and sound now," Amelia said bravely. "It's good to be all back together again, isn't it?"

There was a pause and then they all chorused together,

"But where's Tom?"

"He was with us at the bonfire," Sameer said. "He was standing near me when the firework display started."

"Yes, but what happened to him after that?" Jill asked anxiously. "Perhaps he was injured by one of the exploding fireworks. He might be lying out there all alone and injured."

"We've got to find him," Sameer said, "come on everybody!"

To the astonishment of the adults all six children leapt up at the same time and rushed out of the tent.

"Hey! Come back," someone called, but only Jim returned to grab a torch.

"We've just got to do something," he called, "we'll be back soon."

He soon caught up with the others as they hurried back towards the bonfire. When they got there Jim shone the torch on the remains of the fire to reveal a sorry sight of soggy, black ashes. The stewards had made sure there were going to be no more accidents and had poured buckets and buckets of water over it.

"It looks so sad now," Jill said, "and it was so beautiful and magnificent when it was burning."

"Never mind about that," Sameer said, "wherever is Tom? There's no sign of him at all."

"Oh no, what if he's been burned to pieces?" wailed Amelia.

Jim felt as though the bottom of his stomach had dropped out and he began to panic. Where ever could Tom be?

"Tom! Tom!" he called. "Where are you?" He flashed his torch all around and the children followed its beam calling and calling. Jim circled the fire once and then moved further out into the dark field, the others following. Just as they were beginning to think that Tom was lost forever, they saw a dark bundle in the torch's beam. It was rocking backwards and forwards and making muffled sounds.

"Tom!" they all shouted and ran towards him. They saw he was lying on his side, shivering uncontrollably. His ankles were tied together, tape was stretched tightly across his mouth and tears were streaming down his filthy face.

"Oh Tom, who's done this to you?" wailed Amelia. "Oh, you poor thing!"

"Out of the way!" a man's voice commanded. "Let us through."

The children realised that they had been followed from the tent and as they watched, one of the stewards carefully peeled the tape from Tom's mouth and another unfastened his ankles.

"It's ok lad, you're safe now. We're going to carry you back and we've already called an ambulance, you've probably got hypothermia."

"Does anybody know how long he's been lying here and who's done this?" asked one of the men grimly. "This is really serious."

"He disappeared just before the fireworks exploded so it's not been too long," Jim said, "and I think it was the man who stole the cash boxes and threw the fireworks on the fire. We were trying to catch him and we nearly got him before, but he escaped."

"Whatever were you thinking of?" asked one of the men sternly. "What made you think you could catch him by yourselves? This man is a serious criminal; he's a dangerous man already wanted by the police."

"Never mind that now," the other man said, "let's get this boy warmed up and into an ambulance." They gently picked Tom up and carefully carried him back towards the first-aid tent. The five Fern Valley Venturers followed slowly behind in a sad and sorry state. Shock was settling on them as they realised their narrow escapes from the exploding fireworks and from a dangerous criminal, and now that they were safe, they started to feel very tired and rather weak and wobbly. But then suddenly Jill said brightly, "Well at least Ali will be in the clear now; I wonder where he is?"

"He was with Mr Saunders, remember?" Jackie answered.

"Yes, but when Mr Saunders caught the thief, where was Ali then?" Sameer wondered.

"We'd better go and find out," Jim said; "come on let's hurry up."

Nearly everyone had gone home. The stalls and tents were being dismantled and everything looked messy and depressing. The first-aid tent was still intact and two paramedics were carrying Tom out of it to the waiting ambulance. He was wrapped in a big sheet of silver foil and looked small and pale but gave them a cheery wave.

"See you soon," he called, "cheer up, you all look so miserable but we've caught the thief and got the money back; mission accomplished!"

They watched as Tom's stretcher was loaded into the ambulance and the doors shut. It drove off quickly but there was no siren or blue flashing light.

"I suppose that means he's not an emergency," Jill said, "and that's a relief."

"But where's Ali?" asked Jackie, "Do you think he's gone home already?"

"No, here he is!" Mr Saunders said as he walked towards the children, his hand resting lightly on Ali's shoulder.

"Oh, Ali, are you alright? I can't believe Mr Saunders thought you were the thief," Jill burst out.

"Yes, how could you, Mr Saunders?" Jackie added rather rudely, "You know Ali would never do anything like that."

Mr Saunders smiled sadly at the children and said, "Yes, I do know that. I made a terrible mistake and accused a completely innocent boy and I'm very sorry. I took Ali to the Baby and Toddler crèche to be kept an eye on by one of the women there. I don't know if that was even worse for him than being accused of being a thief! As I was coming out of the tent I could see a man running towards me very fast. He looked as though he was trying to run away so I stopped him. Two cash boxes fell out of his coat pockets and I realised I had caught your thief. We called the police and handed him over to them."

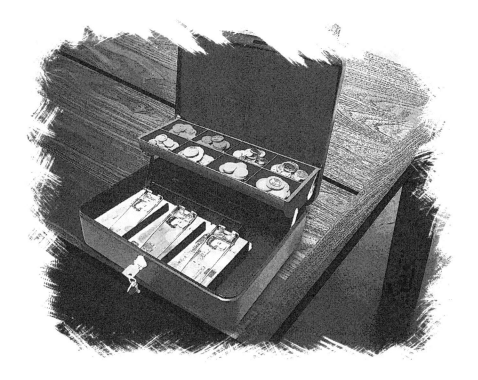

"Gosh, well done Mr Saunders!" Amelia said.

"But what about apologising to Ali?" Sameer asked boldly, "After all, what you did to him was very bad."

"You're right, it was terrible and I have already told Ali I am really sorry. He's very kindly already forgiven me for accusing him of being a thief, as well as for leaving him in a tent with a dozen crying babies and toddlers!"

"Gosh, Ali, have you really forgiven him? If the thief hadn't been caught, Mr Saunders would have had you carried off to the police station and questioned," Jim asked.

"Well yes, he was really, really sorry and I knew he'd just made a mistake so it's all forgiven and forgotten," Ali answered cheerfully. "Even that time with those awful babies is forgiven!"

Then they all saw Mr Jones striding towards them waving and smiling.

"Well done children, thank you for all your amazing help! It's too late tonight but I'll want to hear all about it from you on Monday morning." Then spotting Mr Saunders his face changed and he raised his voice,

"Ah, Mr Saunders, I want a word with you too. I believe you parked your battered old Skoda in my car parking space twice last week and I'm not having it. That space is clearly marked *Headmaster*, so kindly park somewhere else in future!"

"But my car is a battered old Ford, Mr Jones. It wasn't me who parked in your space," Mr Saunders protested.

"Stuff and nonsense, I can tell the difference between a Skoda and a Ford any day, so don't do it again please," Mr Jones said, walking towards his smart new Mercedes, "Good night everyone."

"Well it really wasn't me," shrugged Mr Saunders laughing, "but never mind. Ali has forgiven me a lot today so I think I can forgive Mr Jones his little mistake. After all, I've learnt a lot from what happened to Laura."

"Yes," said Jim, "I think we could all do with learning that lesson!"

"She knows she deserved her punishment from Mr Jones," Amelia remarked, "and she told me she was quite pleased he had been completely fair with her."

"Poor Laura," sighed Jackie, "fancy missing out on tonight's adventures. I hope there was something good to watch on telly instead!"

"Me too, "said Jill, "come on, I'll race you all home!"

Can you tell that The Verdict is a modern retelling of The Parable of The Unmerciful Servant?

Check out Matthew 18 verses 23-34 in the Bible to see what you think.

The hidden meaning of the parable is that God will forgive every wrong thing we will ever do if we ask him. He wants us to forgive the small things that people do to us.

* Do you know that God has already done everything to make it possible for us to be friends with him?

Printed in Great Britain
by Amazon